Demon City

A NOVEL

Morgan Richter

Published in the United States by Luft Books, New York.

ISBN 978-0-9909367-0-1

Cover painting by Elsbeth Monnett

To Auntie Elsbeth and Monkey Joe.

"You've been spending time with Sparky Mother. You have his mark on you, and it's getting you into trouble." She raised her eyebrows over the rims of her glasses. "You don't have to confirm or deny that. I don't need details."

"I've met Sparky Mother twice, very briefly. He didn't mark me."

The icy stare bored into him once more. "He gave you his phone number, didn't he? And you called him. And when you did, a connection was established between you. You became important." She almost seemed to be speaking to herself. "Someone else knew about that call, someone who wants what Sparky has."

"And what's that?"

"Hollywood." She smiled. "Isn't that what most people in this town want? Glamour and power and fame? Sparky's the key to all that." A shrug. "It often comes with a cost, of course. I imagine you've found that out for yourself already."

—*Excerpt from* Wrong City *(2013)*

CHAPTER ONE

IN HINDSIGHT, FELIX absolutely should've asked her about the sex tape. Going into the interview, he'd meant to bring it up; it was even written, in code, on the list of questions on his tablet ("*Do you have any hobbies?*"). But when the right moment came, when he was seated in a canvas chair across from Kelsey Kirkpatrick, a gigantic *Frozen Inferno* poster hanging on the wall behind them, when he'd thought he was ready to broach the subject in a professional yet compassionate manner, he'd stared at that pretty, babyish face with those enormous cornflower eyes, and his nerve had fled. Instead of launching into an interrogation ("*What can you say about the video of you boinking your bodyguard? Did someone steal it from your phone and distribute it online, or did you, as widely rumored, release it yourself with the intention of drumming up a little free publicity?*"), he'd read off the question as it was written, and Kelsey had blinked once at him, those wide eyes a little blanker than usual, before launching into an anecdote about a messy kiln mishap while taking a pottery class in Santa Monica.

Right after the interview had ended, he'd felt okay about it. Kelsey had seemed to like him. She'd even given him a quick goodbye hug, wrapping her tiny pale arms around his neck and enveloping him in a scented cloud of caramel corn and jasmine. Avoiding an uncomfortable topic had been the right approach, he'd thought. But now, sitting on his high, narrow stool in *The Big*

1

Boom's studio, feeling his face melt off from the glare of the lights, he knew he'd made a bad miscalculation.

He was in no position to be making miscalculations.

Tasha finished her piece on Taura Trejo's upcoming Malibu wedding, then Robb smarmed his way through a segment on Paragon Dufresne's unexpected Emmy nomination for her performance in Lifetime's Kylie Minogue biopic, and now Felix was up. He smiled into the lens of the correct camera and read a couple of introductory lines off of the teleprompter, and then his piece began to roll.

He was getting better at interviewing. He watched himself chat with Kelsey on a monitor placed on the studio floor. He looked good on camera, friendly and relaxed. When he first started at Atomic, Curt used to get on his case about how his eyes looked panicky and his smile looked strangled, like his family was being held hostage by armed maniacs somewhere just off camera, and Felix had worked on that, had really, really tried to loosen up. He'd made progress. It probably wouldn't be *enough* progress, but everyone at the network should realize he'd made an effort.

Did his face look puffy? A little, maybe. Chipmunk cheeks. He'd had sushi before the interview, and maybe that was the problem. Jurgen at Pumped! told him soy sauce made him bloat.

Kelsey Kirkpatrick was an easy interview subject, bright and agreeable. In response to Felix's softball questions, she nattered on about *Frozen Inferno*—an action-thriller in which she played a singularly improbable climatologist struggling to expose a vast conspiracy about global warming—as well as her earlier work, like her role on the cult television series *Interstellar Boys* and her breakthrough part in Nickelodeon's *Tweeners*.

Michael had been a *Tweeners* addict, back when they were kids. Michael was Kelsey's age, and he'd nursed a terrible crush

2

on her. He'd once emailed a heartfelt mash note to her agent in the hopes it would reach her. Three years older and much worldlier, Felix had mocked his baby brother mercilessly for that. When he'd looked at Kelsey on the *Frozen Inferno* set, he'd seen the round-faced kid that Michael had adored, and questions about her sex tape stuck in his throat.

He'd watched part of the tape in question. Robb had broadcasted it across the entire bank of monitors hanging on the wall in their newsroom until Tasha had curled her upper lip and snarled at him to shut it off. It was gorgeously lit, all creamy skin and toned bodies and careful angles. It looked less like a porn film and more like some premium-cable production, hitting just the right balance of tawdry and tasteful. Kelsey had gazed straight into the camera, glossy pink lips curled into a calculatedly mischievous grin, and Felix had to look away.

His four-minute taped interview wound down. The stage manager, Duane, crouched beneath the camera and wordlessly counted off the last five seconds on his fingers. The red light on the camera popped back on. They were live.

"Wow," Robb said. "That was some interview, Felix." He smiled, bright and synthetic. The studio lights never penetrated Robb's skin, never made his face melt and his makeup drip the way Felix's always did. Robb slouched on his high stool, hands clasped in a loose ball between his splayed thighs. On his other side, Tasha sat upright, her spine a steel rod, her long legs crossed at the knee. Tasha and Robb were dressed in fire colors: Tasha's sleeveless carmine sheath made her dark brown skin radiate, while Robb's suit was the color of glowing embers. They matched the set for *The Big Boom*, the glossy yellow walls and the tall orange stools.

Felix was the outlier here in his lavender argyle sweater vest. The wardrobe people liked dressing him in schoolboy fashions in candy colors, nothing but sweater vests and pastel cardigans and shrunken seersucker jackets.

"I had a fun time talking with Kelsey. She's a fun girl. And *Frozen Inferno* looks really . . ." His brain shot around for something other than "fun" and finally, inadequately, came up with ". . . cool." Three months at this job, and he still hadn't developed a knack for delivering unscripted banter.

"Sure does. Great stuff." Robb smirked at him, then faced the camera. "We'll have more of Felix's conversation with Kelsey later in the week. When we come back after the break, Jenny Sharp will continue our supercharged pre-Emmy coverage with her chat with two-time nominee Marissa Kestleman."

A jaunty musical sting paired with a stylized cartoon rendition of a mushroom cloud decimating a cluster of skyscrapers marked the start of the commercial break. Before Felix could slide off his stool, the sound guy, Teddy, sprang forward and slipped his hands inside the neck of his shirt to unhook his microphone.

"Jesus, Dockweiler, did you really forget to ask her about the sex tape?" Robb asked.

"I couldn't find a way to work it into the conversation. It never seemed appropriate to bring it up," Felix said. The studio lights blazed above his head, while the rest of the room was in total darkness. He could hear people bustling about in front of him, crew members and production assistants gearing up for the next segment, but he saw only faint silhouettes and flickers of movements.

"Appropriate." Robb snorted. "For Christ's sake, kid, *appropriate* never comes into question here. *Appropriate* isn't appropriate. Whenever a hot teen slut makes a sex tape and releases it to coincide with the opening of her first big movie, we're going to ask her some questions about it. There's nothing tricky about that."

Tasha leaned across Robb to address Felix, bending at the waist while keeping her spine rigid. "Did Kelsey or her people tell you not to mention the tape, Felix?" she asked.

There was a way out. He could say yes, he'd been cautioned against bringing it up, and that would be the end of the issue. No one would call Kelsey's publicist to double-check his story, and Felix would be off the hook. "No. No one said anything."

"Of course they didn't. Because she wanted you to talk about it." That was Curt, their showrunner, stepping out of the blackness to address Felix. His headset was on, and he held a clipboard containing his marked-up copy of the shooting script. "She wants the publicity, the *Frozen Inferno* money guys sure as hell want the publicity, and we want the ratings. It would've been a win-win all around. Okay?"

"Are we sure she leaked the tape herself, though?" Felix asked. "I mean, she says someone hacked her phone. If she's embarrassed about it . . ."

"In the unlikely—*highly* unlikely—event that's the case, it makes no difference. We report celebrity news. If you're talking to a celebrity, you ask them about the news. Right?"

"Yeah. Sorry."

"Does it matter?" Tasha sounded like she was already sick of the topic. "How many leaked celebrity sex tapes have we reported on over the past few years? At this point, it's passé."

"You're speaking for yourself." Robb winked. "Just because you find hot teen sluts passé doesn't mean the rest of us don't have a bottomless appetite for them, chocolate mama."

Tasha turned to stare at him, and Felix could almost swear he felt a chilly breeze in the cramped, overheated studio. She held up a manicured index finger in warning. "Don't."

"What, I can't give my favorite co-anchor a fun nickname?"

"Not if you want to keep your job." Her expression didn't change. It sounded less like a threat and more like a cold statement of fact.

"Yeah? You so sure you could get me fired?" Robb grinned, wide and oily. "I've still got two years on my contract, ladycakes. You're reaching your expiration date, and I haven't heard anyone say anything about a renewal. You might be keeping baby Felix company in the unemployment line."

"Robb, put a lid on it," Curt said. "Felix, tell me you're saving some juicy bits for the second part of your interview."

"Oh, yeah. There's a ton of good stuff. We had a really interesting conversation." He'd talked to Kelsey for twenty minutes before her publicist had shooed him away, and he'd used up all the strongest parts in today's show. Thursday's segment would be pieced together from the dregs.

But that was something to worry about later. Duane called out a one-minute warning, and Robb and Tasha settled back onto their stools. Done for the day, Felix moved out of the lights into the darkness.

"Raise your game, Felix," Curt called after him. "Nobody expects you to be perfect, but you can't botch the easy stuff, okay?"

"I know. Sorry," he said.

Jenny strode by him, cool and sleek in a sleeveless crimson blouse and skinny black cigarette pants. She placed a hand on his upper arm as she passed and gave it a quick squeeze. "I thought you did a great job, Felix," she whispered before hopping up on the stool he'd just abandoned.

It sounded sincere. Jenny was friendly and generous. Jenny could afford to be generous. By the end of the month, barring a miracle, Felix's job would be hers.

He slipped out of the studio before they returned from the commercial break. His chest felt tight and cramped, like a panic attack was coming on at the thought of losing all of this.

CHAPTER TWO

COAL WAS LOCATED in the basement of a rundown building in Los Feliz along a cluttered stretch of Vermont Avenue. Felix made his way through a mass of clubgoers on the back patio and headed toward the unmarked entrance. He could hear the steady thump of music emanating from the interior, a thump he recognized from countless late-night practice sessions. Canary Red was already onstage.

He fought his way down a narrow staircase jam-packed with people. The main room of the club was a cavernous low-ceilinged chamber with a dance floor in the middle and benches and small tables lining the walls. The stage at the far end was a raised platform surrounded by gigantic wall-mounted speakers. It was too far away and too dark to see much, but Felix could just make out the spiky top of Jamie's thatch of peroxide-white hair bobbing above the throng of dancers. Good crowd, lots of people. Good news for Jamie's band, which was burning out a boisterous acid-rock cover of Spandau Ballet's "True."

It wasn't Felix's type of club—too dark, too dirty, not in any way glamorous—but after three months of living with Jamie, he was curious to hear Canary Red perform for a live audience. He wedged himself into an empty spot between two occupied barstools and ordered a cherry vodka seltzer.

The woman sitting beside Felix swiveled around on her stool to face the stage, bumping her knees against his legs in the process. She smiled at him in apology, then jutted her chin in the direction of the band. "They're good, aren't they?"

"Yeah, they sound great." Felix was relieved it was the truth. It shouldn't surprise him, as Jamie appeared to be good at everything he did.

She gave him a quick once-over, then shifted on her stool. "Here. We can share," she said.

"Thanks." Felix perched on the offered half of her seat. It put his hip in direct contact with hers, which, from his perspective, was not a problem at all. The thigh pressed up against his was long and lean and clad in tight white denim; high-heeled sandals were anchored to her feet with a tangle of thin straps and shiny silver buckles. She wore a tight-fitting black t-shirt emblazoned with some kind of intricate, spidery silver logo. Her hair was dark and glossy and fell in wispy razor-cut edges around her face. "Can I buy you a drink?" he asked.

She shook her head, her hair sliding back and forth across her cheekbones, and tapped a pointy silver fingernail against the rim of her martini glass. "I'm all set. Thanks, though."

She stared at him for a moment, her brow furrowing. "I know you, don't I? Do you work at Paramount? Kimber's assistant?"

"I'm on TV. Atomic. I'm a correspondent on *The Big Boom*."

Her expression lightened. "Sure. You're the new guy, aren't you? You've got a silly name."

"Felix Dockweiler."

"That's it." She smiled. "I bet they've suggested changing it, right?"

Nobody had, and Felix didn't think his name was all that silly. "Not yet, but I haven't been there very long."

"They're doing that thing where they're auditioning you on the air, right? You and that dark-haired girl from KTLA. And viewers get to vote for which one of you they like better?"

"You can vote on the website, but I don't think it really counts for anything. It's just kind of a poll, I guess. The producers will decide at the end of summer whether they keep me or Jenny."

"They'll pick you," she said, with the air of someone who had inside information. "She's a better reporter than you are, but you're prettier. All the middle-aged women who sit around watching celebrity news, I bet they go crazy over you."

"I hope you're right," Felix said. No sense in getting offended by her confident assertion that Jenny was better than he was, since it was closer to a fact than an opinion. "It's hard to know where I stand."

"Count on it. Housewives from somewhere in the flyovers don't want to look at some skinny big-city girl on TV. A cute boy like you, that's probably more their speed." She took a sip of her martini, the corners of her wide mouth curling up in what seemed like contempt.

Felix finished his drink in silence. He'd been out of Nebraska long enough that slurs against the flyover states shouldn't hold much sting, but all the same, her derisive attitude irked him. He was considering mounting a defense when she smiled at him again. Minus the scorn, she had a lovely smile. "Sorry. I'm pissing you off, aren't I? I can be a little unfiltered at times." She extended her hand. "I'm Shelley."

"Nice to meet you, Shelley." They shook.

"I came here tonight because I heard the band might be worth watching. Glad I came." She looked back at the stage. "You know anything about them? I work in PR. Are they signed?"

"They're signed. Sony. Their album will be coming out in January," Felix said. "My roommate's the lead singer."

"Really? He's hot." She glanced at the stage, then back at Felix. She winked. "So am I wasting my time with you?"

It took Felix a moment to get her meaning. "Oh. No. No, we just live together. Separate rooms. I didn't even know him before I moved in."

"You're blushing. That's cute," she said. "You're not from here, are you? Are you a Midwest boy?"

"I've lived in L.A. for two years. Before that, I was in New York." He probably sounded a little defensive. He probably had reason to be defensive. "I grew up in Omaha."

"Omaha. I knew it." She dipped two fingers into her martini glass and fished out an olive, then plopped it on her tongue. She chewed it thoughtfully. "I've never been anywhere in the Midwest. Omaha, Ohio, Iowa, Idaho, all those states are one big vowel-laden blur."

Felix opened his mouth, then closed it. Shelley plunked her empty glass behind her on the bar, glanced around the room, and patted his thigh once. "I'm going to mingle a bit. Nice meeting you, Felix," she said, then slid off their shared stool and slipped into the crowd on the dance floor.

He felt a pang of regret at that. Even though she'd made him feel like a hick, she'd been lovely . . .

His attention was caught by the bartender, who plopped a fresh drink in front of him. Felix stared at it in confusion. "I didn't—"

"That's from me." A young woman who'd been seated on Shelley's other side smiled at him. "Sorry. I was eavesdropping." She raised her glass, which contained something the color and consistency of sea foam. "I thought we could toast the great state of Omaha." Her eyes glittered with amusement.

Felix laughed. "Thank you." He picked up his fresh drink, clinked it against hers, and sipped. Vodka and seltzer wasn't ever going to be his favorite combination, but it was low in calories. "I had no idea what to say to that."

"You handled it well. I would've told her off for her smug coastal elitism," she said. "I haven't been here very long, and I'm already sick of how everyone treats Midwesterners like yokels."

The noise level was such that Felix had to lean close to hear her. "Where are you from?" he asked.

"Doesn't matter. I'm here now," she said. "I'm Claire. You said your name was Felix, right? And I heard you say you do something on TV?"

Claire. Claire was a knockout. She had pale hair, stick-straight with a thick sheaf of bangs. Translucent skin and huge eyes that matched the color of her drink. She wore a backless violet blouse with dangling sleeves. She leaned forward and rested her elbows on the bar, careful not to trail her sleeves through somebody's spilled beer, and took a long sip from her glass. Her jeans were cut low, well beneath her hips. With a concerted effort, Felix wrenched his attention away from the clear glimpse of her rear cleavage.

"I'm an entertainment reporter at the Atomic network. *The Big Boom.* I used to model in New York, but I moved out here to go into acting."

"Oh, wow. That's really cool," Claire said. Her enthusiasm seemed genuine, which was refreshing; Felix was used to his career ambitions being met with polite indifference. "I think I want to be an actress. I mean, I know I do, that's why I moved here, but it seems so hard to break in. That's amazing that you're doing so well."

"I'm not, not really. I don't even know how much longer I'll have the Atomic job. It might just be temporary."

"I bet you're great on camera. You've got the face for it," she said.

She nodded over toward the other end of the bar. Felix followed her gaze and saw Shelley, who was now seated at one of the small tables lining the wall, deep in conversation with a pretty young blond man. Shelley was laughing at something he had said, her head thrown back, her hair a dark shining mass about her shoulders.

Claire motioned with her glass toward Shelley. "She's gorgeous. Sophisticated. That the kind of woman you go for?"

"I go for all kinds of women. I might be a little easy." Christ. Had he really said that? That was the vodka talking.

Claire laughed. Good, she seemed to find him delightful instead of idiotic. She smiled and took his hand. Her skin was dry and hot, like one of the chemical hand-warmers he'd slip into his gloves on the way to school on cold Nebraska mornings. "Then finish your drink, and let's hit the dance floor."

Felix danced like a white boy from Omaha. "Sure." He gulped down the rest of his vodka seltzer and slid off the barstool.

She led him away from the bar. Gyrating bodies shoved against him. It was a young crowd, around his own age but several degrees hipper, a sea of artfully disheveled haircuts and thousand-dollar shoes paired with ragged black t-shirts featuring the names of bands unknown to Felix.

Jamie's band was playing something upbeat. Damn. He'd have a better chance of disguising his lack of dancing skills on a slow song. Claire shifted her grip to his wrist and half-dragged him to the center of the dance floor. When they reached a small clearing, she raised her arms and placed them around his neck. Felix slipped his arms around her slim waist and clasped his hands across the warm, bare skin of her back.

Slow dancing to a fast song, then. Much better.

Or maybe they wouldn't be dancing at all. Without warning, Claire leaned in and kissed him. She attacked his lips with surprising fervor. Felix barely had the presence of mind to open his mouth to let her tongue slide in.

She drew back and smiled at him. "You taste like cherries," she said.

There didn't seem to be much to say to that, so Felix stayed quiet and returned the kiss. She pressed close against him. One of her hands dropped down from his neck and stroked along his back until it reached the waistband of his jeans. It slipped inside and worked its way across his lower back to his hipbone. Again, that strange warmth radiated from her touch. It was almost uncomfortable, though unquestionably arousing, especially when she squeezed his hip.

A little startled, he kept his hands fastened around her waist. She drew back from the kiss and moved her lips along his jaw line.

"You're lovely, Felix," she said close to his ear. "Do you want to get out of here?" The hand on his neck moved down his chest and rested on his abdomen.

"Uh-huh," he managed to say.

She smiled, an almost cruel curve to her lips. "Come on." She took his hand again, entwining her fingers in his, and maneuvered him toward the exit.

He was glad they were leaving. He wasn't sure when it had become so overheated in here; he'd been hit by a blast of frosty air-conditioning when he'd first stepped inside Coal an hour or so ago. All the writhing, hot-blooded bodies on the dance floor must've driven the temperature up, because now he felt flushed, almost feverish. Claire's hand was still abnormally hot, and the tighter she clutched him, the warmer he felt.

The walls of Coal were covered in wrinkled black wallpaper shot through with thin lines of metallic orange that glinted from the overhead lights. Felix was reminded of backyard summer barbeques, his dad throwing lighter fluid on charcoal briquettes, the flames leaping up and licking at the metal grill. That had been in the early days when his dad was still around, before things like lighter fluid had been permanently banned from the Dockweiler household.

Claire smiled back at him. She released his hand—a sudden relief, as the heat had grown almost painful—and slid her arm around his waist. "Come on, lovely," she said, her words almost lost in the noise of the crowd and the music.

Her arm was a radiator, pulsing with dry heat. Felix reflexively tried to pull away, then stumbled over his feet as one of the clubgoers collided into him. His center of gravity seemed to be shifting.

Maybe that wasn't such a surprise. He'd only had two drinks, but he hadn't eaten dinner, and he'd gone straight to Pumped! for an hour of cardio after leaving Atomic. Alcohol affected him more when he was dehydrated.

"Careful," Claire told him, her voice filled with laughter.

15

She dragged him up the stairs to the exit. It was a warm, dark, stuffy summer night, and the starless sky glowed a radioactive orange from the city lights. "We'll take my car," she said. She started to lead him across the parking lot in back of the building.

Now that he was outside, away from the pounding music and the noise of the crowd, his brain kicked into a higher gear, trying to pinpoint the problem of what, exactly, was wrong right now.

Claire was wrong. She was *hot*, her whole body was unnaturally hot, emitting waves of heat like a furnace. Dehydrated or not, he was far too confused and disoriented right now, considering the relatively small amount he'd had to drink. For the first time, he felt a spike of fuzzy, muddled panic.

He stopped. Claire frowned at him, her arm still around his waist. "Come on, Felix. I'm parked right over there." She jutted her chin at a small gray sedan.

There. Movement. A shape in the backseat, a silhouetted head bobbing down in haste as if to avoid being spotted, but Felix *saw* it, and even in his blurry state, he knew this was a trap.

"I have to go," he said. "I'm sorry, I have to go, I don't feel well." He pulled away. Claire tried to clutch him tighter, but he slithered out of her grip.

There was something new in her eyes, something quick and clever and radiant. "Don't be scared, Felix. I only want to talk to you."

Her hand shot out and seized his wrist. It *burned*, her fingers scorching his skin as though they were made of hot iron. Felix yelped out loud and jerked his arm away.

"You burned me," he said. It came out high and breathless with shock.

Claire held up both hands, fingers spread wide in a conciliatory gesture. "I'm sorry. I do that sometimes. I didn't mean to." She smiled, reassuring and gentle. "I can explain all of this, Felix. Come with me, and I'll tell you everything."

"I have to go," he said again. He'd parked in the lot, but he wasn't in any shape to drive, and anyway, he'd have to pass right by her car with the mysterious figure lurking in the backseat. He spun around and hurried down the alley that led to the sidewalk.

"Felix!" Claire called after him. He didn't look back.

He walked faster, almost running now, touching the alley wall to keep his balance. When he reached the sidewalk, he was relieved to see the usual chaotic bustle of Vermont Avenue at night, people gathering outside sidewalk cafes and bars.

He jaywalked across Vermont, faster and more carelessly than he would've dared under ordinary circumstances. Drivers leaned on their horns and swerved to avoid him. He was too unsteady on his feet right now for this to be a good idea, but he felt better upon reaching the other side, having placed a barrier of fast-moving traffic between himself and Claire. There was a diner here, shabby and reassuringly mundane, its interior blazing with fluorescent lights, and right now it could be his salvation.

He slid into a cracked orange vinyl booth. A stout waitress in a brown shirtwaist dress and a coffee-stained apron flipped a laminated menu down in front of him. "Water to start?"

"Please." He waited while she filled a scratched acrylic tumbler from a metal pitcher. Condensation stood out on the pitcher in millions of tiny droplets. It was stuffy in here, no air conditioning. "Could I get coffee, too? Black. And wheat toast, unbuttered."

She frowned at him. "You want anything instead of butter? Jelly, cream cheese, peanut butter?"

"No, thank you. Just dry."

She smiled a little. "Dry toast, you might as well chew on the menu. Tastes about the same."

"It's fine. I don't mind it. Just dry, please."

She shook her head and walked off. Felix guzzled the water.

He was having a bad reaction to something. He was sweating too much, and he was far too dizzy. That second drink, the one Claire had given him, maybe she'd put something in it, laced it with some drug and lured him out to the parking lot. The idea seemed unreal, but he was sick and getting sicker.

He plunked the empty glass down on the table, rose to his feet, and headed for the restroom in the back of the restaurant. Just a single toilet in a small room that doubled as a broom closet. It was empty, thankfully, so Felix applied the thumb lock on the rickety door, flipped up the toilet seat, knelt down, and forced himself to vomit.

Memories of kneeling on the cold tiles in the bathroom of his old Williamsburg apartment. He didn't have much in his stomach besides water and vodka. He flushed, splashed tap water on his face in front of the huge industrial sink, dried his hands and face on a paper towel, and checked his reflection in the mirror.

He looked okay. His hair was plastered to his forehead with sweat, and he had unsightly pit stains on what had been a freshly-ironed shirt, but he already felt a little better after getting whatever it was out of his system.

He returned to his booth. In his absence, the waitress had left him a thick beige mug of what was almost certainly very bad coffee and a matching beige plate of dry toast. In a show of defiance, she'd placed two foil-wrapped blocks of butter on the rim of the plate.

Felix smiled at the butter. The coffee was burned and bitter, but it helped clear his head a little. He leaned back into the booth and glanced out the window.

There. On the sidewalk across Vermont, right outside the club, there was Claire. It was too dark to see her face, but her long, pale hair was unmistakable. Another person stood beside her, maybe the shadowy figure from the backseat. Felix had the impression of a man, youngish probably, though he couldn't see him in much detail.

They were glowing, that was the weird thing. Claire and the young guy, whoever he was, they both glowed in the night as though lit by some internal light source that radiated out through their skin. Must be some bizarre trick of the streetlights, an effect that faded away even as Felix watched them turn and walk back down the alley.

He looked at his wrist. There was a red, painful welt where Claire had grabbed him. Where she had burned him with her touch.

He shuddered and hunched down into the booth as far as he could.

CHAPTER THREE

JAMIE BEAT HIM home. Felix stayed in the diner for over an hour, sipping coffee until the frightened fog in his head was replaced by caffeine jitters and a low-grade headache hanging around the bridge of his nose. Eventually, he summoned the nerve to once again cross Vermont, walk down the alley to the now almost-vacant parking lot behind Coal, and get in his car.

The duplex was located along the less-posh south fringe of Beverly Hills. He and Jamie shared the top floor of a small Spanish-style house; Jamie owned the building and leased the lower level to a schoolteacher whom Felix rarely saw. He parked in back, where Jamie and one of the members of his band were hauling equipment out of Jamie's hybrid and lugging it up the back stairs.

"Hey, Felix," Jamie said. He was still in his stage clothes, a tattered black vest over his otherwise bare chest and pin-striped trousers hacked off unevenly at the knees. His eyeliner had smudged and ran down his face in sweaty rivulets; his leathery biceps, covered in a blanket of interlocking tattoos that Felix had never been able to decipher, glistened. "Were you at the gig?"

"Yeah. You guys sounded great. It was a really cool set," Felix said.

The band member, who was tall and angular and had a frizzy thicket of dark hair obscuring his eyes, glanced at him and made some kind of scoffing noise, though Felix wasn't sure what he'd said to deserve it. Felix gestured toward the trunk. "Do you need help carrying things?"

"Don't touch my shit," the band member said.

"We've got it covered. Thanks," Jamie said. With both arms wrapped around an enormous amplifier, he gestured with his head at the band member. "Do you know Andreas? Bass. Andreas, Felix. Felix, Andreas."

"Nice to meet you," Felix said. Andreas scoffed again and jostled past him on his way to the stairs. At the top of the steps, Gretchen and Heidi barked at him from behind their collapsible gate.

"Can you get these damn dogs out of here?" Andreas asked.

"Do me a favor and walk the girls?" Jamie asked Felix.

Gretchen and Heidi had yet to warm up to Felix. They hadn't warmed up to anyone but Jamie, as far as Felix could tell. On the handful of occasions he'd taken them out for their constitutional, it had turned into a lopsided battle, with the twin German shepherds outthinking, outmaneuvering, and overpowering him at every turn. "Yeah, sure."

As he headed up the stairs to the back porch, he heard Andreas mutter to Jamie, "Where'd you find the creampuff?"

"Craigslist. Same place I found you." Jamie's tone was amiable but without any particular warmth, neither approving nor disapproving of Andreas's spontaneous contempt for Felix. Jamie liked him well enough, Felix thought—they hadn't had any major disagreements, no raised voices or slammed doors—but then again, Jamie seemed to like everyone well enough, moving through life with a permanent air of laid-back affability.

He retrieved the leashes, which came with attached zippered pouches full of wadded-up poop bags, and clipped them to the dogs' collars. He received a few low growls as a reward for his effort, but it seemed like a token attempt at resistance more than genuine hostility. The dogs tugged him along the sidewalk toward the park.

It was after midnight, but Beverly Hills was emphatically a Good Neighborhood, and the odds of getting robbed or raped or shot seemed low. Still, tonight he felt jumpy. The dogs, bristly and menacing, boosted his confidence. In the event of an attack (*from Claire?*), he didn't count on them to protect him, but they'd sure try to protect themselves, and that would probably be enough to give an assailant second thoughts.

It was a calm night, warm and stuffy and still. The air smelled like wood smoke, as though one of his neighbors had indulged an eccentric whim to light the fireplace in late August. The dogs conducted their usual canine business in the park, then let Felix guide them home without incident.

Andreas had left by the time he returned. Good riddance. Jamie sat on the back steps smoking a joint. Gretchen and Heidi bounded up the stairs and presented their long noses to be petted and nuzzled.

Jamie bent down and pressed his head between theirs. One of the dogs licked the side of his jaw with gusto. "Thanks for taking care of that, Felix," Jamie said.

"No problem." Felix replaced the leashes on a peg on the wall by the open back door.

"Take a seat. Unwind. I think it's cooler outside right now."

Felix sat on the step beside Jamie. Jamie shifted over and passed him the joint. Felix, his brain overloaded and buzzing from too much late-night caffeine and weirdness, took it and inhaled, trying to look like he did this all the time.

"Andreas is an asshole," Jamie said. He shrugged. "He's a damned good bass player, and I do enjoy hanging out with assholes every now and again, but he was being a shit to you. Sorry."

"It doesn't matter," Felix said. He rested his hands on his knees and looked out into the night. The sky was a dark red, interrupted by the silhouettes of the tall, spiky palm trees lining Doheny Drive. "Do you smell smoke?"

"Wildfires near Malibu. They've been burning all day. That's why the sky is that color. Did you see the sunset? Looked like fresh blood." Jamie tilted his head back to look up. "You have a good time tonight?"

"Yeah. The performance was great."

"We were okay. I don't know that I love the acoustics in that place, but we did what we could." Jamie glanced at him. Felix wasn't sure how old he was, but the lines on his forehead and the leathery quality to his skin suggested he'd hit his forties a while ago. Could be twice Felix's age, easily. "You seem a little distracted."

"It ended up being a weird evening," Felix said. "I met this girl at the club."

"And yet you're home already, so I guess I know how well that went."

"It got strange." Felix glanced down at his wrist, at the shiny patch where Claire had, incredibly, burned him with her touch. "Has anything really bizarre ever happened to you? Something that just makes no sense?"

"Sure. More often than you'd think. L.A. is a weird city. All kinds of bad hoodoo. The longer you live here, the more

23

examples you see of that." Jamie jostled him lightly in the ribs with his elbow. "So what happened?"

He almost told Jamie about Claire burning him, and about his suspicions that she'd drugged his drink, then reconsidered. Better to stay quiet. Putting everything into words would make it seem real, and right now he wanted to keep it firmly in the realm of the unreal, because that would make it easier to dismiss. He shook his head. "Nothing. I just had too much to drink."

"Been there." Jamie stubbed out the joint on the wooden step. "I'm turning in. It's late, and you have to be up early tomorrow."

"Nope. I have the day off. Jenny and I alternate Wednesdays," Felix said.

"They're still doing that crap, huh?" Jamie said. "Making you jump through hoops before they let you know whether you have the job?"

"Yeah." Felix stared at the silhouetted palms. "I don't think they're going to pick me. I screwed things up today."

"Don't count yourself out yet. As far as you know, it's still anyone's game. And even if they don't choose you, it's not the end of the world." When Felix didn't respond, Jamie gave him another nudge to the ribs. "You know that, right?"

"I know."

"You might know it, but you don't believe it." Jamie rose to his feet and brushed off the back of his hacked-off trousers. He'd paired them with thick-soled mustard-yellow rubber boots that looked like something a sanitation inspector would wear to explore a nuclear waste dump. "You have the day off, you want to help me with the restaurant? I could use your design acumen."

"Sure."

One of the dogs—Heidi or Gretchen, Felix had no way to tell them apart—raised her muzzle into the air, sniffed, and growled under her breath. Jamie frowned and squinted into the darkness, then gave her a reassuring pat on the flank. "Jumpy tonight, lady?"

Jumpy himself, Felix glanced around the back yard. He saw nothing out of order. The detached garage, the avocado tree, the hedge of jasmine separating their property from the adjoining one, the small square of unruly lawn, everything looked as it should. No lurking shadows, no mysteriously glowing people. All the same, he found himself shivering in the warm night air.

CHAPTER FOUR

JAMIE'S RESTAURANT WAS located in a recently-vacated Chinese takeout joint along a hot, bleak stretch of the south end of La Brea, wedged in beside a tire store and a run-down strip mall that featured a check-cashing service and a bail bondsman. He'd already overhauled the exterior, and it looked good, walls of hammered copper sheet metal behind a shade-producing barricade of huge leafy plants in gigantic concrete planters. Today, they were painting the interior a deep sapphire blue. Drop cloths protected the unfinished wood floors. Jamie purchased the building earlier that summer and was in the process of preparing it for reopening, though his concept for what kind of restaurant it should be changed weekly. The current theme, he had just explained to Felix, was Korean.

"Why Korean?" Felix asked. "Is it going to be barbeque, or, what's it called, pho?"

"Pho is Vietnamese, Felix." Jamie saturated his foam roller in his paint tray, then let the excess dribble off before applying it to the wall. "I haven't settled on a menu. I've just hired a chef, this fantastic kid who was working at a pool hall in Koreatown, and he and I will pound it out together. As to why, I like Korean food." He shrugged. "And I'm trying to impress a girl."

Felix grinned. "Ah," he said. He lowered his own roller, climbed off the step ladder, and moved back to take in the entire wall. "Are you sure this is the effect you want?"

Jamie squinted at the wall. "It's not right, is it? The color's looking chalky. I thought the primer would take care of that."

"It's the stucco. The paint has a hard time sticking to it, even with primer. It's probably going to take a lot of coats."

Felix's track shorts and bare legs were splattered with splotches of bright blue. Jamie wore sleek, well-fitting black dress pants cut off somewhere around the calves, paired with a sleeveless t-shirt. Felix squinted at the pants, which, like his legs, were drizzled with paint.

"Are those Prada?" he asked.

Jamie turned to him with a confused look, then glanced down at his pants. "Probably, yeah."

"Why are you painting in Prada trousers? Why are you cutting the legs off of Prada trousers?"

"I didn't like them very much. They were comfortable, but they looked too fussy on me. I forget why I even picked them up. I went through a phase where I thought I needed to look like an adult to meet with investors."

Investors. In addition to the band, Jamie had *projects*, like the restaurant and the duplex and a twelve-unit apartment complex that he owned and managed in West Hollywood. Jamie had a degree from the Wharton School and more entrepreneurial drive than anyone Felix had ever encountered.

"Jamie, are you rich?" he asked, the question popping out before he had a chance to squelch it.

"Yeah. I think the recording contract has boosted me up into the range where no one's going to contradict me if I describe myself as filthy rich."

"Why do you have a roommate?" Felix asked.

"I like people. I like living with different people. It forces me to be more adaptive. Not that you've necessitated all that much adapting. You don't take up much space." Jamie set his foam roller back down in the tray and looked at the open door. Gretchen and Heidi lolled just outside on the pavement, resting in the shade of the leafy plants. "I'm about ready to call it a day. I'm going to go for a stroll with the ladies, then how about I take you to dinner to thank you for your help?"

Felix hesitated. "I should go to the gym," he said.

"So we'll go afterward."

Maybe Felix was imagining it, but it seemed like there was something a little challenging in Jamie's expression. "Ah... sure. Maybe."

Jamie nodded to himself, like he'd just received confirmation of a long-held suspicion. "I've noticed you don't eat." His tone was light.

"You've noticed I don't cook," Felix said. "I do eat. I eat plenty. Just not at home, usually."

"If you say so," Jamie said. "No worries. I'm not your mom. Just wanted to let you know it's tough to keep secrets when you live with someone."

"I don't have secrets. I'm a very uncomplicated person. I mean, I'm an *entertainment reporter*, right? Doesn't that automatically mean I'm shallow?"

Jamie grinned. "Like I said, I'm not your mom." He unhooked the leashes from the doorknob. "Think it over, though. I'm offering free food. I can't speak for you, but I'm in the mood for a steak."

A steak. Goddamn. He couldn't remember the last time he'd had a steak. Omaha, probably, going out with his mom and

Michael. Their special-occasion steakhouse had white tablecloths and oil paintings of foxhounds on the walls, and Felix had thought it was the ritziest place on earth.

Left by himself, Felix bagged up the disposable trays and foam rollers and took them out to the dumpster in back. When he came back inside, he was surprised to see a young couple, a man and a woman, peering through the open doorway.

The young man was handsome and brawny, with longish sandy hair and tanned skin. He was dressed in cargo shorts and a shrunken red polo shirt. His companion . . . Felix's pulse surged for a moment, because at first glance he thought she was Claire, scary Claire from the club, Claire with the burning touch. Same blonde hair, long with a thick sheaf of bangs, but she looked taller than Claire, leaner, more angular. She wore a short white sundress that showed off her long, sleek legs. She wasn't Claire, couldn't be. Just someone who looked remarkably similar.

"Hi. We're not open yet," he said.

"Hi, Felix. Remember me?" the young woman said, and Felix's world became very strange, because his first thought had been right and this was Claire, even if she looked *different* than she had last night.

"Claire?" he asked. He felt a little dizzy, like the world had tilted to the side. "What are you doing here?"

She smiled. Eyes the color of sea foam, big and limpid. "I was going to try to convince you I spotted you through the window while we were strolling by, but . . ." She spread her hands in an apologetic shrug. "Whenever possible, I prefer to tell the truth. We followed you."

He stared at her. "From home? Did you follow me home from the club last night?"

She shook her head, pale blonde hair spilling around her face. "Reverse that. I followed you *to* the club *from* your home last night."

"What's going on?" Felix asked. The confusion was now mixed with a growing adrenaline surge, a mounting tingle that started in his feet and rose up through his thighs, which twitched in anticipation of forthcoming action.

She raised her hands, as if to emphasize her harmlessness. "Nothing bad. We just want to talk to you." She motioned toward the young man. "This is my dear friend Nicky. Nicky, meet Felix. Felix, Nicky."

The young man stared at Felix, his expression flat and cold. "That's him, huh?" he said. He tossed his sandy hair back. His neck was thick; his shoulders were wide. He looked like a former high school quarterback, clean-cut and arrogant. "The little twink doesn't look like much. From all you were saying, I thought he'd really be hot stuff."

"Shush, you. He's darling. And we're not going to hurt him any more than we need to." She smiled at Felix. "Ignore Nicky. He gets a little jealous sometimes."

We're not going to hurt him any more than we need to. Felix barely processed anything she'd said after that. "What do you want?"

The young man made some noise that sounded like a snarl. He knelt beside Jamie's tool box, which propped the front door open, and rummaged through it.

"This isn't going to be a big deal, Felix." Another smile from Claire, sweet and conciliatory. "We just need a little bit of help from you, and then we'll get out of your life forever."

Nicky extracted a wrench from the tool box, chunky and heavy. He hefted it experimentally and slapped it against the palm of his free hand. He rose to his feet. "Why don't you make sure he doesn't go anywhere, Claire?"

They were between him and the front door. Maybe he could make it through the kitchen and out into the alley before Nicky caught him. Felix felt his thighs twitch again, his nervous system giving him every indication that *now* would be an excellent time to make his move.

A chorus of angry barks, familiar and, for once, very welcome. Gretchen and Heidi bounded through the doorway, tugging at their leashes. At the sight of the newcomers, they went apoplectic, snapping and growling and lunging.

At the other end of the leashes, Jamie raised his brows at the sight of Nicky and Claire. He made some soft clucking noise with his tongue, and the dogs quieted down.

He gathered up both leashes in one hand and pressed gently against each collar. Heidi and Gretchen sat back on their haunches, partially blocking the door.

Jamie looked from the newcomers to Felix and back again. "Hi," he said. "What's going on?"

Claire turned her brilliant smile on him. "You're the roommate, right? I'm Claire. Nicky and I are just chatting with Felix," she said.

Jamie looked at her without speaking, then turned his attention to Nicky. "Put that back," he said, his voice very calm. The dogs growled in soft unison to punctuate his statement.

Nicky still held the wrench. "I doubt you could make me," he said.

"Am I going to have to try?"

"Of course not." Claire placed her hand on Nicky's wrist. "Nicky, dear, put it back."

After a long moment, while Felix's brain sifted through every possible outcome of this situation, most of which involved explosions of violence, Nicky scowled and shook his head vigorously, a spasm of anger and frustration. He opened his hand and let the wrench drop back in the toolbox with a loud clunk. "Whatever," he said.

"We'll continue this later, Felix," Claire said. She nodded at Jamie. "Nice to meet you, roommate."

She took Nicky by the arm and steered him toward the door. At first, Jamie looked like he wasn't going to let them pass. He glanced at Felix, then stepped aside. Claire and Nicky squeezed past the dogs, who remained in place, growling softly.

Felix moved to Jamie's shoulder, his legs still shaky and tingly, and watched as Nicky and Claire walked to a car parked on the street. Claire was laughing and talking; Felix couldn't hear her words, but Nicky didn't respond. Nicky glanced back at Felix once, his face a dark glower, and Felix had to resist the urge to flinch away.

They stayed in the doorway until Nicky and Claire had driven off. "Okay, you two. They're gone. You can knock it off," Jamie told Gretchen and Heidi. The low growls finally ceased. "Felix?"

Felix shook his head. "Remember how I told you last night was a little strange?"

"The girl you mentioned?"

He nodded. "Claire. That was her. I don't know the guy. She called him Nicky."

"She followed you here?"

"Yeah. From what she said, it sounds like she's been following me for a while. She trailed me to the club last night."

"Is she a fan? From the show, or maybe that movie you did?"

"It's possible, I guess. I didn't get that impression."

Jamie glanced down at the toolbox. "What do you suppose he was going to do with that wrench?"

"I'm glad I didn't find out," Felix said. "I'm glad you came back when you did. They seemed scared of you."

"*He* wasn't. I think he would've been happy to go through me to get to you, if she hadn't stopped him." Jamie frowned. "You don't know what this is about?"

"Not a clue," Felix said. "She said they needed some help from me, but she didn't say what."

"You want to call the police? She's been following you, she knows where we live, that's not good."

Felix mulled it over. "No police," he said at last. "I don't want news of this getting out."

"Why should it matter? It's not like this will get any media attention. You're not really a celebrity," Jamie said.

"I know. That's not it." Felix exhaled, fear replaced by exhaustion. "Right now, I feel like any little thing might count against me with the job. If the network hears about this, if it starts looking like maybe I have a messy personal life . . ."

"If they wouldn't give you the job because of this, it means they're awful people and you shouldn't want to work for them anyway," Jamie said. "When you said last night was 'weird', maybe it's time to explain that a bit."

"I met Claire at Coal while we were listening to your band. We hit it off, so she suggested going somewhere else. I think she might've put something in my drink, because I got really sick and dizzy. And in the parking lot, she grabbed my arm and . . . she burned me."

33

He showed his wrist to Jamie. The skin was still pink and shiny. The burn hadn't blistered, but it had stung during the night; he'd popped a couple of Tylenols and held a towel-wrapped bundle of ice against it to numb the pain.

"How'd she do that?" Jamie asked.

"That's the thing. Maybe she was holding something hot that I couldn't see, but it seemed like she burned me just with her bare skin."

Jamie looked at him for a long, long time. Jamie's eyes were an eerie pale blue, and when he focused his full attention on Felix, it could get unnerving very quickly. "Huh," he said at last.

Felix glanced out the door at the traffic whizzing by on La Brea. It was a stark, hot day, the sun too low and oppressive in a hazy white sky, dirty with ash and smoke from the wildfires. "I know how it sounds," he said. "But that's what happened."

Jamie shook his head and didn't reply.

CHAPTER FIVE

THE EDITING BAY was still occupied by the time Felix arrived for his session. Donya Kashani looked up from her chair and frowned. "Hi. Are you up now? The system crashed, so Emma's waiting for it to reboot. Sorry."

"I'll come back," Felix said.

She shook her head. "Have a seat. As soon as we're back online, I just need to check my piece to make sure all the edits took, and then I'll be out of your hair."

She patted the chair beside her. Seated in front of them, Emma half-turned and gave Felix a quick wave before returning her attention to the editing console.

Donya smiled at him. "You're one of the new kids, right? *The Big Boom*? I'm Donya."

"*Party at Ground Zero*. I know." Probably everyone at Atomic knew who Donya was. She'd been lured away from the new *PM Magazine* in New York at rumored great expense, and she was Atomic's highest-profile reporter by a wide margin. "I'm Felix."

"You're competing with Jenny Sharp, right?" Donya glanced at him. She was petite and lovely, with soft waves of black hair and huge dark eyes. "Any word who it's going to be?"

"They'll make an announcement at the end of the month. I don't really know which way it's going. She's more experienced than I am."

"She came from KTLA before this, right? I saw her reel. Five years in their newsroom. Not too shabby," Donya said. "What's your background?"

"In reporting? Not extensive. I was hosting a weekly webcast for the Atomic site before this. Celebrity gossip. That's how they picked me for *The Big Boom*. Before that, I was acting, mostly."

"You look familiar. Anything I've seen?"

Felix shrugged. "Some TV work. Nothing big. I was in a movie that came out last spring. *Frat Party USA*?"

Donya smiled at that but didn't comment, which was probably for the best. "Hey, I've been stuck in here all morning. Have they identified the body yet?"

Felix's brain, still wrapped up in thoughts about his sad and feeble film career, couldn't follow the sudden change of subject. "Ah . . . body?"

"On the skywalk. They found a corpse early today. Someone was burned to death. Last I heard, no one knew who it was." A keycard-accessible bridge connected the Atomic offices on the second floor to the adjacent parking garage. As a temporary employee, Felix didn't have access to this shortcut.

"Really?" Felix stared at her. "I guess that's what all the police cars were doing in the parking structure when I arrived."

"Yeah. They found whoever it was right before the morning rush. The skywalk has been closed ever since."

"What happened? Some kind of accident, or . . . ?"

"No idea. I've been shut up in here, and there's not much online yet. I was hoping you'd have fresh information."

In front of them, Emma gave a grunt as the console surged into fresh life. Donya's piece began rolling. It was an interview with Laurie Sparks, the flamboyant young designer-slash-reality star, filmed in what looked like a lavish hotel suite. Laurie and Donya sat beside each other on an overstuffed gold velvet sofa, chatting and giggling like old friends. In the editing bay, Donya leaned forward, elbows resting on the counter, and squinted at the monitor, her brow furrowed, her full attention on her piece.

When it had concluded, Emma turned back to Donya. "You happy with that?"

"What do you think, Felix?" Donya asked.

"It looks great to me," Felix said. Emma paused the footage on a freeze-frame of Laurie's beautiful face. "I've heard he's a nightmare to work with, but he seemed nice."

"He can be an absolute brat. I've met him a couple of times in social situations, though, and underneath all that ego and those affectations, he's a good kid. It's a matter of figuring out how to get through to him. Getting on the same wavelength. Same goes for any interview, really."

"You're really good at this," Felix said. "I don't think I have the hang of it yet."

"It comes with experience," Donya said. "I've seen a couple of your pieces. You're doing fine. You're still rough, but you'll get there."

"I don't know if I'll have enough time to get there," Felix said.

Donya tilted her head to the side, conceding the point. "What are you working on? I can take a look at it, maybe give you some feedback."

"Would you? That'd be great," Felix said. He flipped through his binder, which contained his logs and notes. "I interviewed Kelsey Kirkpatrick on Tuesday. This is supposed to be the second part of my interview, but I didn't have much time with her, and I didn't ask her the right questions, and I think I'm in trouble."

"She's been in the news a lot lately. Teen stardom's latest fallen angel, I think that's the position the media is taking."

"Yeah. And I somehow managed not to ask her about the reason she's been in the news. Everyone's kind of irked at me."

"That sounds about right. Still, failing to ask a young woman about her stolen sex tape isn't going to make many year-end lists of top media blunders. Can I see your logs?"

"Sure." Felix passed her his binder. She flipped through pages, skim-reading the transcript of his interview with Kelsey.

She leaned forward. "Emma, do you have Felix's raw footage? Can you cue it up to the seventeen-minute mark?"

Emma nodded once, fingers flying across the console. Laurie Sparks's pretty face went away, replaced by Kelsey Kirkpatrick's equally decorative one. Kelsey spoke in her high, soft, babyish voice about a recent skydiving escapade: "No one wanted me to do it. But I've got this wild side of me that doesn't shy away from taking risks, even when some people don't approve. Haters gonna hate, right?" On the screen, Kelsey glanced down at her lap, then slid her eyes up to look at Felix, her unseen interviewer, staring at him from beneath a fringe of eyelashes.

"There." Donya flicked one mauve nail toward the monitor. "Look at her expression. Right there, she's giving you your opening to ask about the sex tape, but you're not picking up on her cues. You're just reading off your questions without paying attention to the answers."

Felix squinted at the monitor. "She wanted me to ask her about it?"

"I can't say whether she *wanted* it, but she expected it. She came to the interview fully prepared to bring it up."

"And I missed it," Felix said. He stared at Kelsey on the monitor, so young and vibrant, her expression open and expectant, and wondered if he was ever going to get better at this.

When he returned to the newsroom, Jenny was sitting at their shared cubicle, her laptop propped beside their communal computer, typing away. She glanced up at him and shifted out of the single chair. "Hi, Felix. Take the desk. I can work anywhere."

"You don't have to move for me." This was a pattern they'd fallen into, a curious dance, each making every effort to seem generous and relaxed around the other, acting as though they were wholly unaffected by their summerlong gladiatorial battle. Still, he needed the computer, so he accepted Jenny's offer of the chair. She hoisted herself up onto the desk and sat cross-legged, her laptop perched on her knees, and continued typing.

"Did you hear about the body?" Felix asked.

"Yeah. Isn't that bizarre? You hear who it was?"

He glanced over at her. "They've identified it?"

"Him. Chad Bryson. He worked on *Meltdown!*, one of their interns. He was supposed to arrive at seven this morning to copy scripts. Someone found him on the skywalk a little after that."

The Big Boom's newsroom was adjacent to the *Meltdown!* offices. Felix thought he might know Chad. Fair-haired college kid, probably not yet out of his teens. "Interns don't have access to the skywalk, do they?"

"Nope. Nobody knows why he was there. Nobody knows what happened to him."

"Spontaneous combustion. That's what I'm betting on. The kid was charbroiled." Curt paused beside their cubicle. "I envy the trashy gossip sites, what with all the *Meltdown!* jokes they'll get to make. Dockweiler, you get that Kirkpatrick piece sorted out?"

"Yeah. It's in good shape." Donya had stuck with him through the first part of his editing session, collaborating with Emma to piece together his segment. The end result was slicker than he'd thought possible, based on his clumsy, paltry footage. "Do you want to see it before we go on air?"

"Nah." Curt nodded at Jenny. "How're you coming on the *Frozen Inferno* red carpet rundown?"

"Waiting for Graphics to finish the chyrons. I'll check how they're doing," she said. She closed her laptop and slid off the desk, then gave Felix a pat on his shoulder. "See you later, Felix."

Curt plunked down a thin sheaf of papers on Felix's keyboard. "I printed these off of the website. We've been giving viewers a chance to leave comments about you and Jenny. Take a look through them. Might give you some idea of what you should improve."

"Great. Thanks," Felix said.

"No problemo." Curt winked at him and headed in the direction of his office.

Felix picked up the sheaf and began to read the top page. For a long time, he was very still.

His cubicle was right outside Tasha's office. Mesmerized by the printout, Felix didn't notice when she got up from her desk, came out of her office, and stood behind his chair. He jumped when she took the papers out of his hands and dropped them in his trash bin.

"Don't read that crap, Felix," she said. She sounded angry, and at first Felix had the crazy sense that she was mad at him.

She'd so rarely spoken to him outside of the studio that her sudden attention was almost shocking.

"Curt told me to," he said.

"I'll bet he did." The words were sharp. She glanced in the direction of Curt's open office door and lowered her voice. "Nothing can be gained by looking at those."

"If I'm really doing that badly here, it's probably good for me to know what to work on," Felix said. He tried to sound nonchalant, like the comments hadn't shaken him.

Tasha scowled. "The viewer comments on our website are an open sewer. You should know better."

She started to head back to her office. "Tasha? Am I really that awful?" Felix asked.

She turned around. Her brows pulled together. "If you're fishing for compliments, find someone else. I don't play those games."

"I wasn't . . ." Felix trailed off. In all honestly, he *had* been fishing for a compliment, a kind word or two to soothe his bruised ego after the blast of invective-laden vitriol from the viewer comments, and he should've known better than to look to Tasha for that.

"Dockweiler!" Curt popped his head out of his office. He gestured with his phone at Felix. "Loudon Strong wants to see you. His office, now."

Tasha froze. Her expression of irritation shifted into a kind of startled blankness, like she'd just received troubling news that her brain hadn't yet managed to process. "What does Loudon want with Felix?" she asked. It was sharp.

"Who's Loudon Strong?" Felix asked.

Curt barked out an incredulous laugh. "I'm going to pretend you didn't just ask me that, buddy."

"He's the president and founder of the company, Felix," Tasha said. "Curt, did he say what he wanted?"

Curt shrugged. "Greg in his office just said he should go up there when he's got a moment. Which means now, Dockweiler."

"Okay. Where's his office?" Felix asked.

"I'll take you," Tasha said.

"I don't think he needs a babysitter," Curt said. "Even Dockweiler should be able to take an elevator without getting lost along the way."

"I'll go. I need to talk to Loudon myself." She pulled her office door shut and nodded at Felix. "Are you coming?"

Felix hurried to log off of the computer. "Sure, yeah." Atomic's founder. Might be something good, might be something bad. Tasha's obvious surprise at Loudon Strong's request was hard to interpret.

It wasn't just surprise, he realized. Tasha was *shocked* that Strong had asked to see him, unpleasantly shocked. It was tough to figure out what that meant.

CHAPTER SIX

TASHA WAS SILENT in the elevator up to the eighteenth floor. Felix wanted to ask her about Loudon Strong, but her stiff posture, her arms crossed over her chest, the firm line of her mouth, all of it indicated that conversation was discouraged.

The elevators opened into Atomic's corporate headquarters. Softly glowing pale orange walls were emblazoned with a gigantic mushroom cloud of hammered bronze that rose outward in multiple three-dimensional layers. Crimson leather chairs and copper end tables were arranged in a cluster beneath the mushroom. Behind a tall reception desk, a pretty young man wearing a wireless headset flashed perfect teeth at the new arrivals.

"Hi, Tasha. You're here for Loudon?"

"Loudon wanted to see Felix," Tasha said. "If he's free, I'd like to speak to him afterwards."

"Sure, no problem. You want me to call you when he's ready?"

Tasha shook her head. "I'll wait here until he's through with Felix."

The pretty young man looked surprised at that, his sculpted brows sailing up his smooth forehead, but he bobbed his head and flashed his teeth again. "Sure, no problem," he said again.

He tapped a few buttons on the switchboard in front of him and murmured something unintelligible into his headset, then graced Tasha and Felix with another dazzling smile. "Take a seat for a sec, okay?"

"Thank you, Gregory." Without another look at Felix, Tasha strode over to the waiting area, her heels clicking on the stone floor. She arranged herself on one of the chairs, picked up a magazine seemingly at random from one of the tiny copper tables, and began to read it in earnest.

Felix sat beside her. The chair was uncomfortable, and somewhere along the way he'd started sweating, his pink button-down shirt clinging to the small of his back. He did a discreet check for pit stains. Ick. He'd have to make sure not to raise his arms during the meeting.

"Felix?" A gaunt, wraithlike middle-aged woman in a tai-lored red suit hovered to the right of the reception desk. When Felix glanced up, she crooked a skinny finger at him. "I'll take you to see Mr. Strong now."

Tasha looked up expectantly. The woman smiled at her. "Tasha, Loudon said to go ahead and come in as soon as Felix leaves."

Tasha nodded. She still looked displeased about something, but that was pretty much Tasha's default expression whenever television cameras weren't pointed at her, so Felix wasn't sure whether that was significant.

The gaunt woman led Felix down a short hallway lined with gigantic framed posters of the network's current lineup: *Meltdown!*, *Party At Ground Zero*, *The Big Boom*, *Radioactive*, *Fallout*.

Loudon Strong's office had tall double doors covered in glossy black lacquer with a discreet bronze nameplate located to the right. The gaunt woman knocked softly, then pulled open both doors at once. She gestured for Felix to enter.

It was a corner office, and it was huge, almost the size of the whole *Big Boom* studio. Floor-to-ceiling windows took up two walls, providing a panoramic view of the Hollywood hills. The sky was white with a diffuse brown band at the horizon, evidence of the wildfires that were still consuming Malibu; Felix looked to the west, toward the ocean, and saw nothing but haze, the familiar city skyline swallowed up in smoke.

Loudon Strong rose to meet him. He was young, mid-thirties at the most, and he looked familiar, like Felix had seen his photo online multiple times without ever registering who he was. He had short curly hair, his hairline already receding into a sharp widow's peak, and a narrow, friendly face. He wore a bright blue t-shirt emblazoned with the Atomic logo in reflective gold under a dark tailored suit jacket. When he came around from behind his long black desk to shake hands, Felix saw he was wearing jeans.

"Thanks, Liz," he said to the tall woman. She gave him a tight smile and retreated, closing the doors behind her.

"Felix. Loudon. Good to see you." His handshake was firm. "Take a seat."

In lieu of traditional client chairs, a bronze leather loveseat faced Loudon's desk. Felix perched on the edge of it. The leather felt stiff, like it was unused to being touched, much less sat upon. A blast of icy air conditioning caused the sweat on his back to seize up into clammy puddles.

Loudon settled behind his desk again and rested his clasped hands on the surface. He smiled. "Hope I'm not dragging you away from anything important."

"Not at all," Felix said.

"This isn't anything vital. It just occurred to me this morning that I hadn't taken the opportunity to talk to you yet, which seemed like a pretty bad oversight. I mean, if you're going to be here for a while, you should probably meet the whole Atomic family."

"It's nice to meet you," Felix said. "Ah . . . I don't think it's been decided that I'm going to be here past this month."

Loudon waved this away. He had small, nimble hands with fingernails that had been buffed until they gleamed like chips of glass. "I hear good things," he said. He winked, the movement so fast that Felix might've imagined it.

Good things. That was nice to hear. Felix felt a rare glimmer of optimism. Maybe he wasn't as badly outclassed by Jenny as he'd suspected; maybe the purpose of this meeting was to let Felix know he was still very much a contender. Maybe he was even the lead candidate.

He glanced around the office. The walls were covered with shimmering bronze fabric instead of wallpaper. Leafy potted palms unfurled their fronds near the windows. Loudon Strong's wide desktop was bare except for a leather blotter, a phone, and a thin, flat, white cardboard box. The box was battered and dirty, incongruous in this otherwise sleek environment. It had a printed label affixed to the side, which presumably listed the contents, though Felix couldn't read it from where he sat. No computer. The office was devoid of anything that suggested any work actually got done in here, save for a tall, sagging pile of similar thin white cardboard boxes stacked on the black marble floor beside the desk.

Loudon shifted in his chair. He straightened the blotter in front of him, then picked up the box on his desk and placed it on top of the ones on the floor. Something inside the box rolled around and thumped at the movement. If Felix squinted, he could read the label: *Tasha Drummond.*

Noticing Felix's attention, Loudon grinned. He gestured at the boxes. "Those are talent contracts. A bunch are coming up for renewal at the end of the summer, so I've been taking a look through them. Maybe soon we'll have a box for you as well."

"I'd like that," Felix said. "This job has been a dream come true for me, really. I love it here." He sounded a little needy. Probably best to pull back on the obvious desperation a bit.

"I was just looking at your original application. You're from, where is it, Oklahoma?" Loudon asked.

"Nebraska. I grew up in Omaha."

"Nebraska, sure," Loudon said. "Close to your family?"

It would probably be a good move to answer in the affirmative, so Felix nodded. "Absolutely, yeah. Very close."

"Your family still there? In Omaha?"

"My mom is."

Loudon's stare was intense, earnest, riveted. "Siblings? You've got a brother, right?"

Had that been on his application? "Yep."

"Older, younger?"

"He's three years younger." Felix paused. "He's a sopho-more at Northwestern."

"Good school. He must be smart." Something about Lou-don had clicked into sharper focus, like he'd picked up on Felix's faint reluctance to talk about Michael and concluded there might be something interesting and/or juicy there.

"Yep. He is."

"Northwestern. Their school year probably hasn't started yet, huh? Does he spend the summers in, where is it, Evanston, or does he still live with your mom in Omaha?"

"He has a summer job in Chicago." For the life of him, Felix couldn't remember what it was. Retail? Waiting tables? They'd exchanged emails at the start of the summer, right after Felix got the Atomic gig, but their back-and-forth communication had petered out shortly after that.

"You going to make it home for Christmas?"

"I don't know yet. I haven't thought about it. I kind of doubt it."

"Maybe your mom and your brother can come out to see you, hmm?"

"Maybe. We haven't discussed it yet." Why had he been summoned up here for chit-chat about his holiday plans?

Loudon wriggled in his chair. He smiled, splitting that narrow face in two. He looked like a kid when he smiled, inquisitive and precocious. "Sorry. I get nosy about everyone's personal lives. You don't mind, do you? I'm an only child, so I'm fascinated with other people's families. You go to college?"

"Ah . . . no. I moved to New York after high school," Felix said.

"Modeling, right? I think I saw that on your application."

"Well, my initial plan was to get into broadcasting right away." That was an outright lie; prior to submitting an audition tape for Atomic's webcast position earlier that year, he'd never thought much about becoming a reporter. "But I couldn't seem to break in, so I did some modeling to pay the bills. Acting, too. I moved here two years ago hoping the job market would be better."

"Tough field. But it seems to be working out pretty well for you."

"So far, yeah." The conversation stilled. Loudon still stared at him, intense and expectant, so Felix found himself talking to fill the void, saying the first thing that came to his head. "Do they know anything more about the intern?"

Loudon looked blank at first, then he raised his eyebrows and nodded. "Oh, right. The burned kid. Craig?"

"I think his name was Chad," Felix said.

"Chad. No one knows anything yet. God, terrible stuff. Scary." Loudon gave a theatrical shudder. "Gives me the creeps just thinking about it, if someone deliberately set him on fire or whatever. I get to my office at seven every morning, going right across that skywalk. The police say it probably happened not long after that. If I'd arrived a little bit later, that could've been me."

He mulled this over while Felix wondered whether some kind of sympathetic response was required. In the stillness of the room, he heard a faint rattle, like the central air conditioning was breaking down.

It took him a minute to realize the rattle wasn't coming from the ceiling vents. It came from the stack of boxes beside Loudon's desk. Felix looked over at them and frowned.

Loudon grinned at Felix. "Switching gears to something a little less gloomy, I'm throwing an end-of-summer shindig at my home on Sunday. It's a yearly event. All the top talent usually shows up. It's a good time. You in?"

Top talent. Felix was top talent. "Absolutely, yeah. Thanks."

"I'll have Gregory email you my address." Loudon grinned again, then pushed his chair back and rose to his feet. "Well, look, I don't really have that much else to add, so I'll let you go now. Really nice touching base with you."

"You too. Nice to meet you." They shook hands.

"You can find your way out, right? And tell Tasha to come on in whenever she's ready."

Tasha still sat in the reception area. She hadn't moved, as far as Felix could tell, her legs crossed at the knee, looking cold and composed and elegant. She glanced up as Felix approached, then put her magazine aside and rose to her feet.

"He says you can go in," Felix said.

She inclined her chin. "What did he want to see you for?" she asked. It was sharp, almost interrogative.

"He just wanted to meet me. That's all."

Tasha's brow furrowed, and suddenly Felix got it. She was worried that he might, after all, be offered the job. It probably wasn't anything personal, but Tasha was a perfectionist, and she took the show seriously, and thus she naturally preferred Jenny, who was smarter, smoother, *better*.

The realization stung, but there was nothing he could do about that. Tasha frowned at him once more and strode off toward Loudon's office. Felix took the elevator down to the newsroom.

Jenny was at their shared cubicle again when he arrived. She sat on the desk, chatting with the occupant of the single chair. Some kid with pale brown hair, dressed too casually for the newsroom in a t-shirt and jeans. Felix figured it was one of their interns, and then the kid glanced up, and he felt a surge of confusion.

"Hey, Felix, look who showed up in the lobby," Jenny said.

"Hi, Felix," the kid said.

Felix stared at him. "Michael," he said at last.

CHAPTER SEVEN

"WHAT ARE YOU doing here?" Felix asked.

"Nice welcome." Michael shrugged. "I had some free time before the semester starts. So I hopped on a bus and came to see you. Surprise."

"Security called from the lobby looking for you. They said Michael was downstairs. I told them to go ahead and send him up." Jenny looked from Felix to Michael, her expression sharpening, like she was picking up on strange vibes in the air. "I hope that was cool."

"Of course." Felix stared at his brother, his brain trying to adjust to seeing him in this environment. "You took a bus?"

"Yep. Took almost three days. Wasn't pretty, but it was cheap." Michael prodded the dirty backpack on the floor with his Converse-clad foot. "I can crash with you for a couple of days, right?"

"A couple of days should be okay," Felix said. "Some warning would've been nice I've got a roommate."

"If he doesn't want me around, I'll find a motel. It's no big deal." Michael shrugged again.

Jenny cleared her throat. "You're in school, Michael?"

"Yeah. Northwestern. I'm the smart one, Felix is the pretty one."

Michael's t-shirt had a grease dribble down the front, and his hair was lank and unwashed. He looked like he wouldn't smell particularly good. "You look like a homeless person," Felix said.

Jenny let out a shocked laugh. "Felix!"

"I repeat: three days on a bus. Even you might start to look a little trampled, brother dearest," Michael said. He looked at Felix, his expression calculating, and Felix braced for whatever was going to come out of his mouth next.

"You look plastic," Michael said at last. "I don't know. Like you're made out of taffy or something, like you'd melt in the heat."

Jenny cleared her throat. "I'm going to take off. I should leave you boys to get caught up."

"Sorry, Jenny. Felix and I insult each other a lot. It doesn't mean anything," Michael said. "Right now, Felix is uptight because he's worried I'm going to mention that the last time I saw him, he had a completely different nose."

Jenny tried to stifle a snort. Felix felt his face grow hot. "Jesus, Michael."

"Sorry," Michael said again, his tone unapologetic. "You got rid of the bump, right?"

"A casting director suggested it might be keeping me from getting parts," Felix said. "It wasn't a big deal."

"Did that casting director cast you in anything after you got it fixed?" Michael asked.

"The next time I came in to read, she said she was overbooked with guys who look like me," Felix said. "I mean, she was probably right that I needed to fix it anyway, so it worked out fine."

"How much did it set you back?" Michael asked.

"Not very much," Felix said. "Look, Jenny and I have to get ready for the show. Why don't you explore Hollywood for a while, then meet me back here at five?"

Michael hesitated. "Can't I watch you?"

"Closed set. No visitors."

"Then can I just hang out at your desk?" He sounded a little desperate. "It's hot and dirty outside, and I'm exhausted from traveling."

"You can't stay here. It's a newsroom." Felix considered. "You can wait downstairs in the lobby. Or you can sit in my car until I'm done."

"How long will that be? I mean, doesn't it take a really long time to film television shows?"

"We're an hour-long live show. It takes exactly an hour to film it. I'll be out of here at five."

"Okay." Michael exhaled. "Sorry for messing up your schedule. It's really good seeing you, Felix."

"Same here," Felix said, and tried to mean it.

"I thought Beverly Hills was supposed to be fancy," Michael said as he looked around the duplex.

"Parts of it are. But a lot of it is just another neighborhood, you know?" Felix hoisted his brother's backpack and led him down the hallway. "My room's the door on the right. Don't be snobby."

"I'm not being a snob. This is tons nicer than where I was staying in Chicago this summer. It's just not what I pictured." Michael glanced around Felix's room. After a month of sleeping on a mattress on the floor, Felix had recently splurged on a real bed and fresh bedding. Flush with cash from *The Big Boom*, he'd painted and decorated, free to spend money on furnishings for the first time in his life. The room looked nice, like a grown adult lived there.

"Take the room. I'll sleep out on the sofa, if Jamie doesn't object."

"Is he going to be okay with me staying here?" Michael asked.

"Probably, yeah. Not much bothers Jamie."

"I should have called you first," Michael said. "Instead of just popping in on you like this. I didn't really think it through. Sorry."

"Why are you here, Michael?" Felix asked. "It's never occurred to you to visit before this. Why now?"

"I wasn't making much money fixing espresso for stockbrokers. I have a few days before I can move back into campus housing, and it was a long summer. Hot and muggy as hell. I got a little lonely, I guess."

Michael looked crumpled and weary, and Felix felt a rare surge of fraternal affection. "You want something to drink?" he asked.

"Sure." Michael trailed him out to the kitchen and watched as he rummaged in the fridge. Felix didn't keep anything on hand, but Jamie always had beer. He pulled out two stubby little bottles with gilt labels covered with scrawled words in a foreign language.

"Do you drink beer?" Felix asked.

"I'm in college, aren't I?" Michael watched as Felix sifted through drawers in search of a bottle opener before finding one magnetically stuck to the fridge. He popped the tops and passed a bottle over. They clinked in a wordless toast and drank.

Michael wrinkled his nose at the taste. "Strong," he said.

"I know. It's from the Czech Republic. Jamie has complex tastes."

"I don't really know much about beer. Mostly I've only had the stuff you get in kegs." Michael looked a little sheepish. "There's one drink I like, I don't remember what it is. I think it's rum, and it's got cherries and pineapple and stuff in it?"

"Mai tais. Yeah. Those are good." A moment of common ground with his baby brother, united in their mutual love of girly drinks.

The front door rattled, signifying Jamie's return. Felix unfastened the chain lock. Because they parked in the back of the building, they only used the front entrance when they were bringing in the mail. Sure enough, Jamie had a stack of letters in his hand. He paused at the sight of Michael. "Hey."

"Jamie, this is Michael. My brother."

"Yeah? Nice to meet you, Mike. Welcome to L.A." He sorted through the pile of mail. "Most of these seem to be yours, Felix. A couple of rent checks, those are mine. Credit card bill, another credit card bill, both yours." He hefted the envelopes. "Heavy. What exactly are you buying these days?"

"A new face, for starters," Michael said.

"Give me those. Thank you," Felix said. He took the bills from Jamie.

"Minimum payments are the devil's candy, Felix," Jamie said solemnly.

Felix ignored that. "Michael's going to be staying a couple days, if that's okay."

"Of course. This is your home, too," Jamie said. "Stay as long as you want, Mike. What brings you to town?"

"Surprise visit," Michael said. "I had a bit of time before classes start."

"Where do you go to school?" Jamie asked. He looked genuinely curious.

"Northwestern. I'm starting my sophomore year," Michael said.

"That's in Chicago? Evanston, right?" Jamie gave Michael an assessing glance, like he'd just received another clue in a mystery he'd been trying to puzzle out. "Fly or drive?"

"Neither. Bus," Michael said. "Three days." He looked proud of himself.

"Hardcore. I'm impressed." Jamie grinned. "You been out here before?"

"Never."

"We'll have to give you the grand tour." Jamie glanced at his watch. "You guys have dinner plans?"

Michael hesitated. "Could we maybe just order in or something? I'm feeling a little bus-lagged, if that's a thing."

Felix glanced at him. Michael seemed agitated, like he'd been back at Atomic when Felix had suggested he explore the neighborhood. Almost like he was scared of going outside.

"We'll take it easy," Jamie said. "We'll go somewhere nearby and make it an early night. Okay?"

"Sure." Michael didn't sound convinced. Jamie looked from Michael to Felix. His expression was hard to pin down, but it looked like he thought there might be something a little odd about the Dockweiler brothers.

They ended up at a gastropub on Melrose. The place was roomy and dark, with high-backed wood booths that could comfortably seat a mid-sized wedding party. Michael ordered a Guinness with his burger and seemed grimly triumphant when the waiter didn't card him. Felix's soy patty came swaddled in multiple layers of romaine in lieu of a bun. Jamie glanced at his plate. "You want any of my fries, grab them."

"Thanks. I'm good," Felix said.

"You sure? I've got plenty to spare."

Michael glanced from Felix to Jamie. "If you've been wondering about Felix's eating habits, I can save you some guesswork," he said. "He was a chunky kid, and then in high school he decided he wanted to be a movie star. So now he overcompensates."

"Shut up, Michael," Felix said.

Michael raised his eyebrows at him. "What? It's true. I didn't say you were anorexic or anything. I was just giving Jamie some background on your complicated relationship with food."

"I eat plenty," Felix said. "Maybe not by Midwest standards, but for Los Angeles, this is a pretty normal dinner."

"Don't bite my head off. I'm not spilling deep, dark family secrets." Michael finished his beer and looked around hopefully for their waiter.

Jamie smiled. He looked bemused by Michael's lack of an internal censor. "Anything good?" he asked.

"Hmm?" Michael turned back to him, frowning.

"Family secrets." Jamie gestured with his head at Felix. "That one doesn't talk about himself much. I figure I should get all the good dirt from you."

"Oh. Yeah. Well, nothing about Felix. Felix was a good kid." The waiter placed another pint glass in front of Michael, black and foamy. Michael leaned forward and slurped at the foam without lifting the glass from the table. "I'm the one with *problems*. I've got a police record."

Jamie shrugged. "Big whoop. So do I," he said.

"Yeah? What's yours for?" Michael asked.

"Drunk and disorderly. Defacing public property. Trespassing. Failure to disperse. I had an outstanding time in college." Jamie swallowed a gigantic bite of his burger. "Your turn."

"Michael, maybe you shouldn't do this," Felix said.

Michael raised his chin. "If I'm going to be a guest in Jamie's home, he should probably know. My reputation as a firebug precedes me," he said. "Two warnings, one arrest, all before I was twelve."

"You're an arsonist?" Jamie asked. His tone was mild, almost bored, as though he were inquiring about an interest in birdwatching.

"No." Michael set his mouth in a firm, grim line. "I don't set fires. None of it was my fault." He picked up his glass and gestured at Felix with it. The contents slopped over the side and splashed on the table. "Felix doesn't believe me. Mom probably doesn't, either. Dad sure didn't."

Jamie was quiet for a while, considering Michael with a faint smile on his lips. "You're an odd bird, Michael," he said.

"I know." He gestured with his head toward Felix. "He didn't tell you he had a brother, right?"

"It hadn't come up in conversation, no."

"You can probably guess, we're not close." Michael considered, shrugged. "Or we are, really, I mean we're brothers, but . . . There are problems, I'll just say that."

"Maybe spending some time together will help you with that," Jamie said. "You taking any time off of work, Felix?"

Felix shook his head. "It's not like I can call in sick whenever I want. If I don't do the show each day, they'll drop me."

He thought Michael looked disappointed, which was oddly touching. "It doesn't matter," Michael said. "I'll probably just hang out at your place and get caught up on sleep."

58

"I'm not doing much tomorrow," Jamie said. "I'll show you around. We can do all the tourist crap, hit the beach, go see Hollywood, that kind of thing."

"You wouldn't mind?" Felix asked.

"My pleasure," Jamie said. He settled back, draping one long arm over the back of the booth, and observed Michael and Felix. "Might be fun."

Horror and terror and agony, all blended together into one high-pitched sound that ripped through the still night. Felix sprang up from the couch, his fleece blanket tangling around his bare legs, and ran halfway down the hall before he realized he was awake, heading at a breakneck pace toward the source of that too-familiar noise.

From the back porch, Gretchen and Heidi barked, alerting the neighborhood that something was amiss. Felix burst through his bedroom door and fumbled for the overhead light.

Michael sat upright in bed, face white, eyes wide, hair sticking up in all directions. His chest rose and fell. He was shirtless; Felix saw the familiar rubbery circular patch on his chest and had to look away.

"Shit," Michael said. He closed his eyes and took a deep breath. "Shit. I'm sorry."

Felix felt his heart rate subside. He sat on the edge of the bed. "Still having nightmares?" he asked.

"Obviously." Michael exhaled. "It's fine. It's just embarrassing. I'm sorry."

Out back, the dogs continued barking. Their downstairs neighbor probably thought they'd murdered someone up here.

"Felix?" Jamie, shirtless and clad in boxers, stood in the doorway.

"Nightmare," Felix said. "It's okay. Sorry."

"No problem," Jamie said. "Can I get you anything, Michael? Water?"

Michael shook his head. Jamie covered a yawn. "I'm going to calm down the ladies, then. 'Night, guys." He left.

"Do you want me to stay with you?" Felix asked Michael.

Michael shook his head. He looked like he wanted to burst into tears. "Jamie's probably wishing he hadn't agreed to let me stay here."

"I doubt it. I'm sure he understands. Nightmares happen," Felix said.

"You're not thrilled with having me here either, are you?" Michael asked.

"This isn't your fault. I know you can't help it." Felix placed his arm around Michael's shoulders. Michael immediately tensed up, so Felix settled for patting him on the back once, awkwardly, then removing his arm. "Are you in some kind of trouble?"

Michael looked over at him. "No. Why?"

Felix shrugged. "Well, it's weird having you visit me. And you're having nightmares again. And . . ." Felix paused, wondering whether to continue. The image of Claire and Nicky popped into his brain, unbidden.

"And?" Michael asked.

"No one's looking for you, are they?"

"What do you mean?" Michael's eyes were wide.

"I met some people a couple days ago. A man and a woman. It was kind of a weird situation. They said they'd been following me, and I don't know why. Do you know who they were?"

Michael shook his head. "I have no idea what you're talking about."

"Are you sure? They got a little scary, Michael."

"Nothing's wrong," Michael said. "Nobody's looking for me. I'm just exhausted from spending way too long in transit, and I had one of my nightmares. That's all. It's my own fault for talking about old times at dinner. Stirred up some memories. Call it karma for being such an ass to you about your nose."

"If you're sure—"

"I'm sure." Michael flopped back onto the pillows. "Thanks for checking on me, but I just want to go back to sleep." He curled up on his side and yanked the covers up to his ears, indicating the conversation was over.

"I'll be in the living room if you need anything," Felix said.

Michael just ducked his head further under the comforter. Felix stared at him for a while, then flipped off the overhead light and retreated.

The back door was open. Jamie stood at the top of the stairs, still in his boxers, the dogs curled around his ankles. He leaned his forearms on the railing and stared out into the darkness. Felix hesitated, then came out to join him. The night air was warm and smoky.

"Sorry about that," Felix said.

Jamie shook his head. "Your brother okay?"

"I think so." Felix considered how to approach the subject. "He's got some problems."

"I guessed that." Jamie glanced at him. "You want to discuss his penchant for starting fires?"

"It hasn't happened since we were kids," Felix said. "Our parents were going through a bad spell. No money, fighting a lot, that kind of thing. Michael got a little crazy."

"Yeah? Just the fires, or was there something more?"

"Just the fires. Three in a month. His bedroom, the garage, the backyard. No one was hurt, but the fire department had to be called, so the police got involved. Then dad left, and we moved into a smaller place, and Michael's problems stopped. He saw a shrink, a lot of shrinks in fact. They thought he was just acting out."

"Mike says he didn't do any of it, right?"

"He says there were people living inside his body." Jamie threw him a startled look. "People made out of flames. According to Michael, they burned their way out through his chest and started the fires."

"That's weird." Jamie frowned. "That's really weird. That's not what I was expecting. You think it was like a multiple-personality kind of thing?"

"More like a desperate-bid-for-attention kind of thing." Felix felt tired of the subject and a little guilty about discussing Michael's personal history with an outsider. "He set fires, he got caught, and he gave a dumb excuse instead of 'fessing up. He's stuck to that story for so long he probably believes it by now, but it's a bunch of crap. Obviously."

"Mmm." Jamie stared out over the yard. "I read something online about the body they found at your workplace."

His tone was mild. Even still, Felix bristled. "That's unrelated."

"Yeah? Mike showed up at your office, right?"

"He was still on the bus when the intern got killed. It happened in the early morning, and Michael didn't arrive until late afternoon. More to the point, Michael's not violent. He would never attack anyone."

"I'm not suggesting he would," Jamie said. "He doesn't seem like the type. All the same, it might be worth checking to see if there've been any weird fires in Chicago lately."

He crouched down to scratch each dog behind the ears, then straightened up. "Get some sleep, Felix. And think about taking some time off to spend with Michael. Seems like he might need his big brother."

As it turned out, there was no need to take time off. Michael left town the next day. He called Felix at work, his voice drained and distant through a bad connection.

"I asked Jamie to drop me off at Union Station," he said. "I'm boarding a bus in a few minutes. Heading to Chicago, with some weird detours through Texas and Arkansas. I'll be home by Monday."

"I thought you were staying longer," Felix said. Twin pangs of relief and regret fought for dominance.

"I was getting in your way. Jamie was a good sport about it, but I could tell he thought leaving earlier was a good idea too. School's starting soon. It was a dumb idea to come here." Michael fell silent. "Thanks for putting me up, though. And for putting up with me."

"Are you sure you want to do this?" Felix asked. "Tomorrow's Saturday. We could spend all day together."

"The ticket's already bought," Michael said. "Look, I'll call you when I get settled in at campus, okay?"

He disconnected the call, leaving Felix with a strange sense of loss.

CHAPTER EIGHT

LOUDON STRONG'S HOME was located at the end of a twisty drive on the hillside above the Hollywood Reservoir. A guard posted at the gated driveway checked Felix's name against a list and let him park in the horseshoe-shaped courtyard in front of the sleek, sprawling, ultra-modern house.

The heart of the party took place on the back patio, which jutted out over the side of the hill. Felix looked down on the reservoir, the surface calm and shimmering, the lights of the city blanketing the horizon beneath it. To the west, the setting sun glowed red on the horizon, surrounded by an orange sky.

Loudon was deep in conversation with Robb and Curt. Upon spotting Felix, his face lit up with a broad grin. He gestured for him to come over. "Felix! Glad you could make it. Do you have a drink? Let me get you a drink." With a nod at Robb and Curt, both of whom seem surprised to see Felix, he took Felix's arm and steered him over to a hosted bar set up by the railing. "What's your poison? Donnie here makes a fantastic fire-breathing martini. It's tonight theme drink, what with all the wildfires."

"Sounds great." Felix watched as Donnie, the unsmiling bartender, poured jiggers from a series of bottles into a cocktail shaker and shook it ferociously. Jalapeño vodka, cinnamon schnapps, liquid smoke. Felix's stomach lurched.

"Any trouble finding the place? These roads can be a bitch."

"I made a few wrong turns, but I figured it out." Felix's martini came in a stemmed glass the size of a fishbowl and was garnished with a whole charred jalapeño. The first sip was like sucking on a charcoal briquette. "This is a great place. Your view is amazing."

"Not too shabby, is it? It's been a good house for me. This is my big farewell to it." Loudon grinned. His curls were stuck to his forehead with sweat. "The hillside shifted around too much during those storms in May. The earth's still too loose. City inspectors said I'd have to rebuild it or junk it, or the next time it rains, it's going to slide all the way down into the reservoir."

Felix stared at him. "Yikes."

"Relax. We're safe. It never rains in L.A." Loudon winked. "So I'm building this new house out in Malibu. As soon as it's ready, I'll move in there and have this place torn down. No problem, right? Trouble is, the new place is smack dab in the path of the wildfires. How do you like those odds? Get crushed in a mudslide or die in a fire. Which way would you pick?"

"I wouldn't want either," Felix said. He took another cautious sip of his drink. His tongue felt like it was blistering. "I hope your house is going to be okay. Both houses."

Loudon shrugged. "They will or they won't. Out of my hands. Act of God, right?" He craned his neck, looking at the crowd, then patted Felix on the back. "You know pretty much everyone here, right? I don't have to introduce you around, do I?"

"No, I'm good," Felix said.

"Great. Good to see you. Thanks so much for coming." With another pat, Loudon drifted off into the crowd to mingle with his guests.

Left alone, Felix moved over to a vacant space at the railing, taking care not to slosh his monstrous drink. Jenny, elegant and cool in a backless blue jersey dress, sidled up and bumped her shoulder against his. "You went with the fire-breather, huh? You're more of a daredevil than I thought, Dockweiler."

Jenny held a glass of white wine. Felix felt a stab of envy. He was a little disgruntled to see her here, he had to admit. It made total sense that Jenny would be invited as well, but he'd been hoping he was special, that Loudon had summoned him to his office and invited him as an overt show of favoritism. He held up his drink. "I don't think I'm man enough for this."

"Let me try." Jenny leaned over and took a sip from the rim. She scrunched up her nose and scraped her tongue against her top teeth as though trying to remove the flavor from her taste buds. "Huh. Yeah. That's not good."

"Our host says it's the theme drink for tonight." At Jenny's startled look, he gestured at the red horizon. "The wildfires. It still smells smoky out here."

"Ah. Got it. For a second there, I thought Loudon was talking about that poor murdered intern, which would have been in exceptionally bad taste."

"Do they know for sure he was murdered?" Felix asked. "It couldn't have been some bizarre accident or anything, right?"

"The spontaneous combustion theory?" Jenny shook her head. "Doesn't seem likely."

"Any word on why he was on the skywalk?"

"His producer gave him her access card. She takes the bus, so she wasn't using it." Jenny twisted her mouth into a grimace. "Sad, scary story. That poor kid."

"Yeah." It seemed inadequate, but Felix wasn't sure what else to say. He didn't like thinking about it, about poor Chad

Bryson, whose death had indeed spawned a gajillion horrible *Meltdown!* jokes from gossip sites, as Curt had predicted.

Jenny drained her glass. "I'm going for a refill. If you want to ditch that monstrosity, I can get you something better." She took the fishbowl out of his hand.

"Thanks, Jenny." She smiled in reply and nudged her way through the crowd toward the bar.

Left alone again, he looked around. On a shadowy end of the patio, Tasha sat by herself on the edge of a chaise lounge. She wore some kind of black-and-silver sequined jumpsuit that would probably look garish on anyone less inherently elegant. She bent forward and rubbed her bare foot, a high-heeled sandal on the wood floor beside her. He approached.

"Did you hurt your ankle?" he asked.

Tasha glared up at him, as though annoyed at being caught in a moment of weakness, then relaxed. "It's not serious, Felix. My heel got caught between the boards, and I broke a strap." She picked up the ruined shoe and examined it.

"Is there any way to fix it?" Felix asked. "I could ask around for a safety pin or something."

She shook her head. "There's no need. My driving moccasins are in my car." She bent down to unbuckle her other sandal.

She'd have to walk barefoot through the party. "If you give me your keys, I can get your shoes for you," Felix said.

She frowned at him, like she was suspicious of his offer, then rummaged around in her silver clutch and produced a set of keys. "Cream Mercedes convertible. I'm parked on the west side of the courtyard, to the right of the door."

"I'll be right back." Both the patio and Loudon's living room were clogged with party guests. To avoid the crowd, Felix slipped down a steep flight of narrow wooden stairs leading down from the patio to a paved path that inclined up alongside the house. He found Tasha's car in the courtyard and retrieved a pair of silver leather loafers from the floor beneath her steering wheel. The interior of her car smelled expensive and complex, like basil and amber.

He made his way back along the same shortcut. As he walked by the side of the house, he glanced through a window and found himself looking into a recreation room. A cluster of partygoers sat on gigantic cushiony sofas in front of a big-screen television, which was broadcasting a boxing match.

Loudon was there, too, standing in the doorway and talking to a sandy-haired young man. Felix froze at that, because it was Nicky, Claire's scary friend.

It was dark outside, and the recreation room was brightly lit, so there was little chance of Nicky spotting him if he looked out. Even so, Felix ducked to the side, safely hidden by the wall, then leaned forward a few inches and peered through the window.

It wasn't Nicky. The young man looked something like him—similar tanned features—but his hair was shorter, and he was much slimmer and sleeker. More sophisticated, somehow, in a charcoal suit with a pale blue shirt beneath it. Felix observed him for a few seconds longer until he was absolutely certain he'd been mistaken. His heart rate fell back to normal.

He hurried back up the steps to the patio. He placed the loafers on the chaise beside Tasha and passed over her keys. "Here you go," he said.

She accepted them without looking at him, a distracted frown on her face. Unthanked and unappreciated, Felix felt snubbed.

She replaced her keys in her clutch and pulled on the shoes, her movements precise and slow. She rose to her feet and discreetly brushed off the back of her jumpsuit, the sandals dangling from one finger by the straps.

"Thank you," she said at last. "That was nice of you."

"No problem. I'm sorry you hurt your foot."

She assessed him silently for a moment. "You'll take this the wrong way, but I don't mean it unkindly," she said. "There's every chance you'll be offered the job, but it won't be a good match for you. I hope you won't accept it."

Felix paused. It was blunt, uncomfortably blunt, even though he'd already sensed Tasha's feelings on the matter. "I know I don't have Jenny's experience," he said.

Tasha shook her head. "It's not only that. You're very rough, but you'll probably improve with time. You've improved some already. But you're too immature for this, and that's a bigger problem. You want the job too much. This is a dangerous place for people who broadcast their desires so openly."

"Atomic is dangerous?"

"I meant Los Angeles. The entertainment industry in general," she said. She sounded irritated. "You're too vulnerable. Out of desperation, you'll make decisions you shouldn't make. If you're not careful, it'll destroy you."

Ah. Tasha was worried he'd turn into a cautionary tale. He wasn't sure which demons she thought were most likely to consume him—drugs? Loose women? Unspecified moral decay?—but in her eyes he was starring in some hackneyed morality play, the callow farm boy from Nebraska bartering his soul for a shot at fame.

Felix had never lived on a farm, and he wasn't quite as naïve as all that, and while he supposed it was nice she thought about him enough to be concerned, he felt a little disgruntled by her assumptions. He smiled to mask his annoyance. "I appreciate you telling me this."

"I know I'm being rude," Tasha said. "You've always seemed like a nice enough boy. But you're wrong for Atomic, and Atomic is wrong for you."

Okay. She'd drilled her point home. Time to end the conversation gracefully and make his retreat. As he searched for the proper parting remarks, she gave him a cool nod. "Take care of yourself, Felix."

She moved into the crowd. Felix stared after her. He started when Jenny approached his shoulder and spoke into his ear. "I thought you'd ditched me, Dockweiler." She handed him a glass of white wine. "This might be more your speed."

"Perfect. Thanks."

Jenny pointed with her chin in the direction of Tasha's retreating back. "So I saw all that. Tell me that woman didn't ask you to fetch her slippers."

"She didn't. I offered to fetch them myself."

"Yeah? Judging from your expression, I'm guessing she wasn't sufficiently grateful."

"She told me she doesn't want me to get the job."

"She didn't." Jenny's eyes widened. "Balls. That was rude of her."

"She said she didn't mean it in a unkind way." Felix shrugged. "It seemed pretty unkind."

"You think?" Jenny took a sip of her wine, her dark eyes thoughtful. "It's going to be you, you know. That's what I keep hearing."

"I've been hearing exactly the opposite."

"You're beautiful, Felix. You look great on camera. And when you're reporting on something, you look so earnest, or

70

involved, or something. You look like you *care*. People want you to succeed."

"I believe Tasha described the way I look as 'desperate'." He smiled at her. "Thanks, though. I could use the pep talk."

"Either way, it really doesn't matter. Whatever way it goes, we'll both be okay. We're too good not to be." She clinked her glass against his. "To us."

"To us." Felix drank. "Robb mentioned the other day that Tasha's contract expires soon. He sort of implied that renewal wasn't a sure thing."

"Robb would say that, because Robb's a dick and he can't stand that she makes so much more money than he does." Jenny considered. "Might be true, though. She's been with Atomic from the start, and I'd say they'd be idiots to get rid of her, but who knows? After all the money they spent hiring Donya Kashani, management might be looking for ways to trim some fat from the budget. Tasha's got a solid fan base, but she's a middle-aged woman in a field that values youth over experience. She's still a knockout, obviously, but you know she's turning fifty this year?"

Felix hadn't known, but he could believe it. Tasha was smooth-skinned and well-preserved, but there was a gravitas to her that reeked of life experience.

From behind Jenny, he saw the young man from the recreation room again, the one who looked so much like Nicky, angling through the crowd, making his way to the railing. His eyes met Felix's.

The young man smirked and raised two fingers to his forehead in an ironic salute, and Felix realized he'd been wrong, that his memory had been playing tricks on him, because he clearly *was* Nicky.

Sensing his sudden distraction, Jenny glanced over her shoulder and saw Nicky's retreating back as he melted into the crowd. "Someone you know?" she asked.

Felix shook his head and swallowed hard, aware of a sudden uncomfortable tightness in his chest, like the lingering ashes in the air were clumping together in his lungs. "No," he said. "I have no idea who he is."

CHAPTER NINE

GRETCHEN AND HEIDI started barking at him from the back porch before he was even halfway up the stairs. They thrust their muzzles over the edge of the collapsible pet gate and bared their teeth at him. Felix froze. "Easy, ladies," he said. "Nice doggies."

The nice doggies were unappeased. They growled and snapped. Jamie had promised him, flat-out swore to him, that Gretchen and Heidi knew he was benign and thus would never, ever bite him, so he took a deep breath, squared his shoulders, and nudged his way through the gate. The dogs growled, but true to Jamie's promise, they didn't attack.

Once inside, he could smell the smoke from the wildfires clinging to his clothes and hair. Gross. He needed a shower and a good night's sleep.

Light streamed from beneath his closed bedroom door. It was possible Jamie had entered his room for some reason, though it was far more likely Felix had forgotten to switch his lamp off before leaving for the party. He opened his door.

Claire sprawled on her stomach on his bed, leafing through the most recent issue of *Details*. She looked up at him and smiled.

"Hi, sweetheart," she said. "Close the door, would you? We're going to have a little talk."

Felix stared at her, frozen in the doorway. "What are you doing here?"

His closet door was open. The greater part of his wardrobe was heaped in a pile on the floor. Nicky stepped out of the closet. He wore a jacket, Felix's favorite suit coat that he'd bought with his first paycheck from Atomic. It was lightweight wool, black with a cobalt silk lining, and even though it was usually too warm in Los Angeles to wear it, Felix loved it dearly

Once again, Nicky had changed his appearance. He was even taller and slimmer than he'd been at the party. His hair was different too, blonder and styled in a fair approximation of Felix's own cut. He smiled at Felix. "She said close the door."

The flight instinct kicked in with the smile. Felix bolted.

Something hit him from behind. He fell to the floor with Nicky on top of him. A hand gripped the back of his hair and smashed the side of his head into the wall. Bright white spots danced across his vision.

Nicky tangled his hand in the back of Felix's shirt and dragged him back down the hall to his bedroom. When Felix jerked away, Nicky kicked him in the side. He wore Felix's shoes, a shiny black pair of dress loafers. With surprisingly pointy toes, Felix noted for the first time. It was a small mercy that Nicky hadn't raided Jamie's closet, as Jamie favored industrial boots.

Nicky hauled him upright. "Move," he said. He shoved Felix to the bed.

Claire hadn't moved from her position. She looked up from her magazine. "Gently, dear. He's very fragile."

Claire had changed, too. The bangs were gone; her silky blonde hair was now one long length, tied off her face with a patterned silk scarf. She wore jeans, dark denim cut low beneath her hip bones, which protruded from either side of her chiseled abdomen.

She sat up. "Come here, Felix, and sit with me," she said. Her cropped sweater vest rode up as she moved. It was fastened with only one button, revealing a vast stretch of uninterrupted torso.

"What do you want?" Felix asked. Nicky pushed him over to Claire. Felix sat on the edge of the bed, as far away from her as he dared.

"Just to talk, sweetheart. A few little questions." Claire slid over to him and put her arm around his shoulders. She nuzzled her face against his hair.

"You smell like smoke, Felix," she said close to his ear. "I like it."

"He's going to smell a lot more like smoke in a minute," Nicky said. "Smoke and charred meat."

Nicky looked around the room and snorted. As the rest of the duplex had been fully furnished when he'd moved in, Felix had poured all his design energy into his bedroom. The walls were painted toasted almond up to the white crown molding. His bed and dresser were made of dark polished wood, deeper and glossier than the wood floors. Bottle-green velvet curtains matched the plush chenille throw rug. "Christ, it's girly in here. Why don't you get a canopy bed and be done with it?" Nicky looked at Felix. "Little plastic nitwit with your stupid face and fancy clothes. We'll be doing the world a favor by burning you."

"Shut up, Nicky," Claire said. She stroked the back of Felix's hair. "You're scaring Felix."

"You think?" Nicky said. "He should be scared. I'm good at this. That kid at your workplace, you hear about that? That was me." He sat down on the edge of the bed next to Felix. Felix cowered back against Claire. He could feel the outline of her breasts against his back, which under other circumstances would be arousing. "Cute kid. Dumb as all hell. Never knew what hit him. He looked like you, all clean-cut and vacant. That made it better."

Felix flinched. Nicky leaned closer. "It'd been years since we'd killed anyone, hadn't it, Claire? We've been stuck in one place for too long. Not by choice, either." He smiled at Felix, his eyes narrowing. "But finally we're loose. And this time we even made it out of Omaha. I don't need to tell you about Omaha, do I? That place fucking sucks."

Claire stroked Felix's hair again. "Omaha wasn't so bad. I liked it," she said. "But we think Los Angeles suits us so much better. So sparkly and fun. All those pretty, skinny, silly people. But see, the two of us have a built-in expiration date. So in order to get around that, we're going to need to borrow your brother again."

Felix was quiet. Michael. He'd known, *known* this was about Michael, but it was still a jolt to hear it. "Why do you need Michael?" he asked. His voice quavered. Damn it.

There was an odd light in Nicky's eyes, almost a glow. "Because the little nitwit set us loose in the first place," he said. "He can do it again, the next time we need him. But he went rabbit on us, so you're going to tell us where we can find him." He looked over Felix's head at Claire. "I bet he's a screamer. No sense waking the neighbors."

"Right." Claire removed her hand from Felix's hair and slid the scarf off her head. She wrapped the opposite corners around each hand. Felix glanced back to see what she was doing. "What are you—"

"Shh," Claire said. "This won't take long." She slid the scarf over his head and gagged him with it. Felix tried to twist aside, but she leaned back on the bed, pulling him down with her.

Nicky leaned forward. He raised his hand. "Not his face, darling," Claire said.

Nicky snorted. He placed his open palm on Felix's sternum, above the open neckline of his shirt.

It burned. It seared. Nicky's hand was a hot iron against Felix's bare skin. Felix screamed into the scarf and burrowed back against Claire in an attempt to squirm away. Claire clutched onto his shoulders, fingers digging into his skin. He shrieked into the scarf, almost asphyxiating around it, not caring if he did.

After several seconds of agony, Nicky removed his hand and sat back. Claire held on to Felix for a moment longer, then relaxed her grip. Felix lay against her, not struggling as she removed the scarf.

Everything was quiet for a moment, except for the sound of Felix's strangled gasps and the distant howling of Gretchen and Heidi from the back porch. Claire patted his shoulder. "Where's Michael?" she asked in a conversational tone.

Felix shook his head. "He's not here," he said. "He took a bus back to Chicago."

"Bullshit," Nicky said. "He's close. You think we wouldn't know if he left the city?"

Felix cringed against Claire. Claire patted his shoulder again and made some faint conciliatory noise. "He left, that's all I know. I haven't seen him again." Nicky lifted his hand. Felix flinched back. "Please, don't . . ."

Somewhere along the line he had started crying. He closed his eyes as Claire touched his face, wiping away the tears with her thumb. "Hush. It's okay. We believe you. You'd tell us if you knew, wouldn't you, Felix?"

Felix didn't say anything. His shoulders shook. He turned his face away from Nicky and burrowed against Claire. Her arms came up around him. If he'd had anything in his stomach other than the glass of wine at Loudon's party, he would have lost it.

"Doesn't mean we can't have some fun," Nicky said.

"Not with Felix. We might still have some use for him," Claire said. She petted Felix's hair.

Nicky got to his feet. "Sometimes, Claire, you're a major kill-joy."

"Mmm. This one's too pretty to waste, that's all." Claire stroked her hand through Felix's hair once more, then released him. She slid off the bed and rearranged her clothes. She retied the scarf around her hair. "We'll see you around, Felix."

Felix remained frozen in place on the bed, trying to get his sobs under control, until long after he'd heard the front door close. He willed himself to stand and assess his condition.

His side didn't feel all that great from where Nicky had kicked him, and he had a painful bump on his temple in addition to the burn on his chest, but other than that, he was okay. Physically, at least.

He forced himself to leave the bedroom and walk out to the living room. He turned on every light he passed along the way. Claire and Nicky were gone. Good. What was he supposed to do in this situation? He should call the police, shouldn't he? Tell them the whole story, let them take it from here . . . Felix looked down at the hand-shaped burn on his chest where Nicky had touched him, and calling the police no longer seemed like a great option.

They'd left the front door open. Felix shut it. The bottom lock was broken, the wood splintered to pieces around it. He flipped the deadbolt and put on the chain.

At the back of the duplex, something thumped against the back door. He jumped, then stared in the direction of the kitchen, trembling. Another thump. And another. Then a low whine.

He headed for the kitchen. The whine came again, low and insistent. He opened the back door, his fingers taking too long with the locks, and crouched down. He extended a tentative hand. One of the dogs snorfled against it in what seemed like relief.

This was a switch from the disdain the dogs usually showed him. Well, they had warned him not to go into the house, hadn't they? Felix looked down the dark stairs and shuddered.

One of the dogs pushed past him into the kitchen and began to prowl around the apartment. The other stayed by his side, nuzzling against his legs as he closed and locked the door.

He couldn't sleep in his room tonight. He'd stay in the living room and wait for Jamie to come home. Jamie might call him crazy, but then again he might not. He might know what to do, because Felix sure didn't have any idea.

He sank down onto the couch and leaned his head back. The dog, he wished he knew which one, rested her long nose in his lap. He stroked the top of her head.

Jamie might know.

CHAPTER TEN

WORK WAS UNENDURABLE, torturous. Jamie hadn't come home last night. Nothing too unusual about that—Jamie kept weird hours, and he often crashed with friends or members of his band—but Felix had spent an agonizing night on the couch, unable to relax, much less sleep. In the morning, he'd walked the dogs while feeling something approaching terror just from being outside, exposed. He'd left a message for Michael, struggling to keep the panic out of his voice, warning him that some dangerous people were looking for him.

News brought more horror in the form of another burned corpse: Timothy Quinn, twenty-one, aspiring actor, found in an alley behind a nightclub on the Sunset Strip. At his shared cubicle at Atomic, Felix had scrolled through the news article on his computer, his stomach twisting at a photo of Timothy. It was his professional headshot, in which he looked glossy and cute. And now he was dead.

That was almost certainly Nicky's work. He would've been looking to blow off steam after attacking Felix, and Claire would've let him do it. Some of that was on Felix, too, because he hadn't called the police last night. It probably wouldn't have been enough to save Timothy, but at least Felix wouldn't be feeling this crippling cloud of guilt in addition to the low-grade terror.

He sleepwalked through the broadcast. Once it was over, he was free for the day, to return . . . home? That didn't sound too appealing, since apparently Claire and Nicky could break into the duplex without much trouble.

In the makeup room post-show, he removed the heavy layer of paint Kimberly had slathered on him. He had a purpling bruise on his forehead from where Nicky had slammed him into the wall, and another one on his neck from struggling against Claire while Nicky tortured him. Kimberly had used a small brush to apply a thick, sticky layer of concealer over both without asking questions, and Felix hadn't volunteered an explanation.

"Looks like someone showed you a good time last night, Dockweiler." Robb winked at him from the adjacent makeup chair. He squinted close to the mirror and wiped under his eyes with a cream-soaked tissue. Felix stared at him in shock. "You look like a used band-aid. Wouldn't have pegged you for the rough stuff."

Felix couldn't answer, and he couldn't meet Robb's eyes in the mirror, so he didn't say anything. He focused on removing his makeup as fast as he could so he could get the hell out of there.

Robb chuckled. He got to his feet and mussed up Felix's hair on his way out the door. "See you, chocolate mama," he called to the occupant of the final makeup chair.

Tasha ignored Robb. She'd already removed her heavy on-camera makeup and was now reapplying a light coat of eyeliner and mascara.

Felix looked in the mirror. Robb was right. He did look like a used band-aid. His eyes were bloodshot, and the bruises stood out too stark against his pale skin. He lightly touched his chest.

Beneath his shirt, the hand-shaped burn felt warm. He'd sprayed it with an analgesic and taped gauze over it, but it was still painful.

The surface of the burn had turned dark pink and shiny, like the old scar on Michael's chest. Michael had always insisted he'd received it when the people living inside him, the people made of fire, had burned their way out of his body.

People made of fire. Wasn't too hard to figure out who they might be.

"Felix." That was Tasha. He looked up and met her eyes in the mirror. Her face was composed. "My office."

Without waiting for him to reply, she walked out of the room. Felix followed her downstairs from the studio to the newsroom.

She didn't speak or acknowledge him in any way until they were in her office. She shut the door and pointed to a molded plastic chair in front of her desk. "Sit."

Felix perched on the edge, ill at ease.

Her office was small and fastidious, papers neatly filed in labeled metal bins, pens gathered in a matching metal cup. No personal touches, no photos or plants or artwork or knickknacks. It smelled like Tasha's perfume, like basil and amber. A small flat-screen television was mounted to the wall, tuned to the local news but with the sound turned off. She settled into her chair, shifted her computer keyboard into a more comfortable position, and began to type without saying another word to Felix.

Felix waited for her to speak. She ignored him, going about her business as if he weren't there. His attention was drawn to the television, which was soundlessly broadcasting footage of the most recent burning death. Young club kids in their flashy best stood around a parking lot cordoned off with yellow police tape, watching as paramedics loaded a cloth-covered gurney into an ambulance. More photos of Timothy Quinn, probably from his Facebook page. He looked young and vibrant, and it was hard to overlook the fact that he looked not entirely unlike Felix.

"Can I turn that off?" he asked Tasha.

She glanced at the broadcast, then back to him, her eyes narrowing. She nodded He leaned over and pressed the power button. Timothy Quinn vanished. Tasha continued typing.

The tears he'd been suppressing all day finally started to fall, which was splendid timing. He kept his head down and hoped he could pull himself together before Tasha noticed. He looked down at his pants and sniffled as discreetly as he could manage.

He was startled by a movement from Tasha. He glanced up to see her waggling a box of tissues in his direction, her attention still fixed on her computer screen. He took one and dabbed at his face. He kept his head down. He'd never been able to cry attractively. His face was probably puffy and blotchy.

Finally, Tasha spoke. "How did you get the bruises?"

Felix inhaled. It was a little shuddery. "Someone broke into my apartment last night and attacked me," he said.

"Attacked you?" Her voice was calm.

"Beat me up. And burned me." Felix unbuttoned his top button and pulled the collar open to reveal the gauze patch.

Tasha frowned. "Do you know who he was?"

"He was a guest at Loudon's party last night. I'd seen him before. He and a woman, it's the two of them, they're looking for my brother."

"Why?"

"I don't know. Michael gets in trouble a lot. He was visiting me. He already left, but I don't think they believe me that he's gone, and I'm worried they're going to come back."

"I assume you've already gone to the police?"

Felix shook his head. "I didn't call them."

She looked at him, her expression stern. "Even if you're careless about your own safety, I'd think you'd want to protect your brother."

"It's more complicated than that," Felix said. He took a deep breath. "The guy—his name's Nicky—he burned me with his hand. He placed his bare hand against my skin, and my skin burned."

Tasha was silent for a long, long time, looking at him with that same cool, solemn expression, a look that didn't convey compassion or pity or any emotion Felix could easily identify. Maybe a hint of worldly resignation coupled with grim intelligence, but nothing that helped Felix figure out what she was thinking.

Finally, she nodded. "The intern. Chad Bryson?"

"Nicky killed Chad. I'm pretty sure of it. He flat-out told me he did, and I believe him. And I think he killed that other kid, Timothy Quinn, after he left my place last night. The woman, Claire, she wouldn't let him kill me, and that made him angry." Felix's voice broke. He had to stop and compose himself before he could continue. "I know I should tell the police, but there's something really wrong with them. Nicky and Claire. I don't think they're . . ." He trailed off.

"You don't think they're human," Tasha said, her tone flat and expressionless.

"I don't know," Felix said miserably. "It sounds like I'm making it up. They look a little different every time I see them, like their actual bodies keep changing, and they glow in the dark a little, and they can burn people just by touching them."

He sounded high and shrill. Tasha's expression grew wary, like she thought he might go into hysterics. He took a deep breath and tried to get himself under control. "There's got to be a reasonable explanation for it, I know that, but they really scare me."

"You said he was a guest at Loudon's party," Tasha said, like she was steering the conversation back into safer waters.

Felix nodded. "Nicky was talking to Loudon Strong. I saw them together. And I think . . ."

"What do you think, Felix?"

Felix shot a glance at the closed door and lowered his voice. "I think they know each other. I think that's why Loudon asked to see me the other day. He asked me questions about my brother, like where he lived, and it didn't seem too weird at the time, but now . . ."

"I see."

"I don't know if Loudon's involved or anything, but at the very least it seems like he knows Nicky. Maybe he—"

Tasha held up a finger. "Stop. I need to think about this." She was quiet for a long, long time. Finally, she reached for the phone on her desk and punched in an extension. "Gregory, I'm here with Felix Dockweiler. Is Loudon available? Felix has something urgent to discuss with him." Tasha was silent, listening to Greg's reply. She glanced at Felix once. "As a favor to me, Gregory."

She listened for a while longer, then replaced the phone without another word. She looked at Felix.

"Ten o'clock tonight. Loudon's office."

"Ten o'clock?" Felix asked.

"Loudon left the office early on other business today. He'll meet us tonight as a special favor."

85

"You'll be there?"

Tasha nodded. She paused. "There's a need for some caution here, Felix. I'm sure you can appreciate that, but it bears emphasizing. You do not suspect this man—Nicky—of having any connection to Loudon. That idea has never even entered your head. You believe he followed you, uninvited, to the party last night. Am I clear?"

"Yes. You are." For the first time, something other than the usual calm solemnity had entered Tasha's expression. She seemed agitated, which was disconcerting. Was Tasha frightened of Loudon? He was her boss, sure, and as the head of a cable network he probably wielded a fair amount of clout in Los Angeles, but there wasn't anything scary or dangerous about him.

"Tonight, then." Tasha nodded at him in what was a pretty clear dismissal.

"Thank you," Felix said. "Thank you for helping me."

She shook her head. "As I told you last night, I think you're a nice boy." Her mouth drew into a stern line. "And I think you might be venturing into some things that aren't very nice. It makes me worried for you, Felix."

Her and Felix both.

CHAPTER ELEVEN

TASHA WAS WAITING for him in the parking structure, standing beside her Mercedes. Even though it was five minutes before ten, she glanced at her watch and frowned as he pulled into the space beside her.

"Come on," she said without any further greeting.

Felix followed her in silence. The skywalk to the building was still closed, barricaded with a tangled cobweb of yellow police tape. In front of the glass doors was a makeshift memorial to Chad Bryson, bouquets of browning carnations wrapped in ribbon-tied paper, prayer candles in tall glass jars painted with depictions of saints, hand-written letters. Tasha walked straight past the display without sparing it a glance.

In silence, they crossed through the small courtyard and entered the building. They produced their Atomic identification badges at the security booth just inside the door; the night guard scrutinized them for far too long, like he was committing their names and employee ID numbers to memory, then sat back and waved them through to the bank of elevators.

The reception desk on Loudon Strong's floor was unoccupied; the overhead lights were off. The double doors to Loudon's office stood wide open, but the office was dark. Loudon's desk chair was turned around to face the windows. The top of his hair peeked over the back.

Tasha and Felix paused in the doorway. Tasha cleared her throat softly.

The chair swiveled around. "Hi, guys," Loudon said. "Take a seat."

His tone was friendly and natural, and Felix relaxed. He hadn't realized how tense he'd felt about this clandestine night-time meeting.

Even in the darkness, the floor-to-ceiling windows let in enough of the city lights that it was easy to see Loudon. "Flip on the overheads if you want. It's kind of relaxing here in the dark," he said. "Sorry to drag you out here in the middle of the night. I was at a conference across town for most of the afternoon, so I figured I'd come back to the office late to get caught up. It's amazing what I can get done when it's quiet. What's up?"

Felix hesitated, wondering where to start. Tasha answered before he could get his thoughts together. "Felix came to me with a problem, and I suggested you might be the best person to handle it," she said. "Someone who may have been at your party last night apparently followed him home and attacked him."

Nicky hadn't followed him—he and Claire were lying in wait for him, which meant Nicky had left the party before him—but Felix saw no point in contradicting Tasha. Loudon widened his eyes in what seemed to be genuine surprise. "Jesus Christ. That's awful," he said. "Who was it? What happened? You okay?"

"I don't know who he is," Felix said. "I thought maybe you'd be able to help us identify him. I'm pretty sure he doesn't work here."

Loudon was nodding before he finished his sentence. "Sure, yeah, absolutely. What did he look like?"

"He's young. Around my age or maybe younger. He's a white guy. He had sandy hair, fairly short. He was dressed nicely." Felix closed his eyes and tried to picture Nicky. At the duplex, he'd been wearing Felix's own clothes, but at the party . . . "A dark gray suit with a light blue shirt. It looked expensive. No necktie." He swallowed. "I think I might've seen you talking to him inside the house, maybe." Remembering Tasha's earlier caution, he kept his tone deferential.

Loudon frowned, like he was thinking very hard, then nodded. "Okay, yeah, I think I know who you mean. That guy. He said he was a guest of . . . shoot, I can't remember who he came with. I'm not even sure he told me, come to that. He cornered me at some point and tried to pitch me an idea for a reality show, some social experiment about ordinary people becoming famous, something that every network has tried at some point. I turned him down gently, and then I tried to keep away from him for the rest of the party."

Was that the truth? Loudon's expression seemed open and honest, but Felix didn't know his mannerisms well enough to know what he looked like while lying. "Do you remember his name?" he asked.

"He introduced himself as Nick. I didn't get a last name. He tried to give me his card, but I didn't take it. I'll ask the guards who were working my gate, see if they remember who he came with. If that doesn't work, I can make some calls and ask around." Loudon leaned forward in his chair and stared at Felix. "He attacked you? Like, to rob you or what?"

In the darkness beside Felix, Tasha straightened her spine, like she was bracing herself for whatever he was going to say. "I'm not sure. He said a bunch of stuff, but none of it made much sense to me. I think something was mentally wrong with him."

The stack of long, flat boxes Felix had noted before were still piled on the floor beside Loudon's desk. A muted noise came from inside the top box, the one that bore Tasha's name. A muffled rustling, a faint thumping. Felix glanced at it, but neither Tasha nor Loudon seemed to notice.

Loudon shook his head. "Scary stuff. Glad you're okay." He settled back in his chair. "You tell the police about this?"

"Felix wasn't sure that would be a good idea," Tasha said before Felix could speak. "He didn't want to drag the network into any messy news story."

"Well, that was thoughtful of you, Felix. Obviously, though, your safety is more important than a little fuss and bother from the media." Loudon rested his elbows on the smooth surface of his wide desk and pressed his fingertips to his chin, deep in thought. "I suppose our first step is to figure out who this guy is, right? I'll work on that from my end, and once we've got an ID, we can take that to the police. Okay?"

Another noise came from the box. Felix glanced at it. The lid popped up a centimeter or two, as if something had pushed against it from the inside, then fell back down into place.

Neither Loudon nor Tasha reacted to the noise. Felix felt the start of something growing in the pit of his stomach, something akin to fear. He opened his mouth to ask something.

Tasha reached over and, without looking at him, gently closed her hand over his. She gave it a firm squeeze, then released it. Felix closed his mouth.

She rose to her feet. Following her lead, Felix stood as well, his attention still fixed on the box.

"Thank you, Loudon," she said. She smoothed out her crisp white pants and shouldered her purse. "Felix and I appreciate your concern."

"Jeez, no trouble, absolutely." Loudon rose as well. "Tasha, I'm glad to see you've taken Felix under your wing. Seems like he could use a friend these days."

Tasha smiled. It was filled with ice, and for a brief moment she seemed almost dangerous. "We're all friends here, Loudon," she said. "Felix?"

"Thank you," Felix said to Loudon. "Thanks very much. I appreciate it."

"No problem, Felix. Hang in there. We'll get this all sorted out."

Felix's last glimpse of Loudon was of him standing behind his desk, silhouetted in the dark, watching after them as they left.

CHAPTER TWELVE

IN THE ELEVATOR, Felix turned to Tasha. "What—?"

"No." A single syllable, like a gunshot, and Felix fell silent.

They left the building, passing the silent, suspicious security guard at the door. Outside, it was warm and dark and silent. No one was in sight, save for a homeless man sitting on the cobblestones, resting his back against the low cement wall surrounding the cultivated trees in the courtyard. Felix couldn't see much more of him than a mass of tattered garments topped off by a long overcoat.

The homeless man looked up as they passed, and Felix realized he was a woman. Asian, short hair bleached almost white, two inches of dark roots standing out against her skull. Her right eye was misshapen, the corner pulling down toward her ear. She was missing an arm, the empty right sleeve of her overcoat pinned up to her shoulder. She noticed Felix's attention and scowled at him, her expression violent, and Felix looked away.

In the parking structure, his car wouldn't start. Not a terrible surprise; it was a bona fide clunker, the dashboard held together with a mighty wad of duct tape. If he was offered the job—a big if, bigger every day—he could splurge on something new. The engine wouldn't turn over, not even a small sputter of life to give him hope that maybe it would eventually start if he kept at it.

Tasha sat in her own car, parked in the space next to him, her head down, engine off. Maybe she was switching into her silver driving moccasins. Maybe—Felix hated to entertain the thought—maybe she was waiting for him to leave so she could continue her talk with Loudon.

She rolled down her window and gestured for him to do the same. "What's wrong?"

"My car won't start. It does this sometimes," he said. He stared at the entrance to the skywalk, at the rows of police tape, and tried not to feel nervous at the prospect of waiting for a cab by himself in the darkness.

Tasha hesitated, her mouth scrunched into a frown. "I'll take you home."

"Which direction are you going?" Felix asked.

"I live in Baldwin Hills."

He wasn't entirely certain where that was, but he had the impression it was to the south, somewhere around the sprawl of low hills and oil wells he always passed on the way to the airport. "I'm in Beverly Hills. That's the opposite way, right?"

"It doesn't matter," Tasha said. She looked around the dark, deserted parking garage and shook her head in what looked like resignation. "Get in."

It was clear she didn't want to give him a ride, and under other circumstances Felix would gracefully turn her down. Considering recent events, he couldn't climb into the passenger seat fast enough. "Thank you. Sorry to make you go out of your way."

She frowned at him. "Put on your seatbelt."

They drove west. The Atomic building was on the east end of Sunset, close to the entrance to the Hollywood Freeway. Felix stared out the windows at trendy restaurants nestled alongside boarded-up buildings and ratty old storefronts.

Tasha gestured out the window at a local television station. "Five years ago, that's where I was. Spent almost two decades there, started as an entertainment reporter and worked my way up to anchoring the six o'clock news."

Felix knew this, but it seemed like Tasha was talking almost to herself, so he said nothing. She shook her head and continued, staring straight ahead. "I grew up here. In Los Angeles, I mean, but it could've been the other side of the moon. Compton. You ever been to Compton, Felix?"

"No, I haven't."

"I don't suppose you have." A grim smile. "You don't get details, I don't know you well enough for that, but getting out of there wasn't exactly the easiest thing I've ever done. But I did it, and I did well for myself. Still, though, I always had my eye on making the jump to national. L.A. is a big city, but local news is still local news."

"Is that why you took the job at Atomic?" Felix asked.

She ignored him. "So five years ago, my husband Tony, he had an aneurysm. I found him in the den when I got home from work, television tuned to the news. He'd been watching me when it happened." She smiled at that, quick and bleak.

"I'm sorry," Felix said.

"Just one of those damn things," she said. "Then a couple of months later, my contract came up for renewal, and I got the axe. Back when I was young and cute, I'd replaced someone older, and now someone younger and cuter was bumping me out of my slot. Call it the television circle of life." She shook her head. "I wasn't sure I was ever going to work in television again. That's when Atomic came along."

She smiled again. "Answer to a few prayers, that place. It was just starting up, and Loudon hired me himself. It was a good move. I don't think it's too arrogant to say I helped lend it some respectability during those rough first couple of years, back when everyone had us pegged as some trashy E! knockoff. And in return, the job pays me a lot. An awful lot."

Felix had no idea where this was heading. The scenery flew by. They'd reached the Strip now, and they'd passed La Cienega, which was the best place to make the turn toward his place, but he didn't want to interrupt her narrative.

"My contract with Atomic is a little strange, Felix. Not everybody has one like it, but it's what I was offered, and I agreed to it with open eyes. After Tony passed, I was feeling reckless and angry, and maybe a little desperate. It's easy to look back now and see that maybe I should have been more careful, but you know what? I wasn't careful. And I don't know if it matters. Everything has turned out pretty well for me, and there's no reason to think it won't continue that way."

She was quiet. Felix cleared his throat. "You should take a left here," he said. "What was strange about your contract?"

She glanced at him. "Like I said, I don't know that it matters," she said. "But my fear is that it's the kind of contract you're likely to be offered, because you seem so hungry for this job that you'd take anything, and I doubt it'd turn out as well for you."

"And if the job goes to Jenny?"

"I don't worry about Jenny. She's smarter than you are. You're the one at risk."

"What was in the boxes?" Felix asked. "In Loudon's office, I heard noises coming from the box with your contract in it. You heard it, too."

She shook her head. "I don't know what you mean."

95

They were silent for the rest of the trip, the stillness broken only by Tasha occasionally asking directions. She dropped him off in front of the duplex.

As he slid out of the seat, Tasha stopped him. She gripped his forearm, nails digging into his shirt, holding him in place. He looked at her in shock.

"If he calls you, or contacts you in any way, let me know," she said. Her expression was grim, her tone angry. "Under no circumstance do you agree to anything without telling me first. Anything at all, do you understand?"

Felix didn't understand much of anything that had happened that night, but he figured the only way to get Tasha to release his arm was to agree. "Yes. I understand," he said. He nodded for emphasis.

Tasha examined his face, then let him go. She sat behind the wheel and stared straight ahead, waiting while he got out of the car.

He hesitated on the sidewalk, holding onto the open passenger-side door. "I don't really know what's going on, but thank you for helping me."

She didn't look at him and didn't answer. He closed the door, and she drove off into the night.

The chain lock might be on the front door, so Felix walked down the driveway to the back entrance. The dogs weren't at the top of the stairs, which meant they were either inside with Jamie, or Jamie was taking them out for a walk. Either way, it meant Jamie was probably around, which was good news.

The dogs were on Felix as soon as he pushed open the door. They exploded into a cacophony of barking at the sight of him. Felix froze in the open doorway, certain he was about to get mauled.

"Gretchen! Heidi! Knock it off." Barefoot and bare-chested, his tattoos revealed in all their splendor, Jamie popped into the kitchen, looking stable and comforting. He grabbed hold of the dogs, one hand on each collar, and hauled them back. They surged forward, barking and growling at Felix.

Jamie nodded at Felix before he could say anything. "Change out of your clothes. In fact, shower. They smell something on you." He almost had to shout over the noise of the dogs.

"We need to talk. Things have been happening—"

"I know. I saw the broken lock on the front door. Shower first. It'll be quieter if we can talk without the girls bawling you out." Jamie jerked his head in the general direction of the bathroom. "Now. Throw your clothes outside the door." When Felix didn't move, frozen in place by fear and surprise, Jamie huffed in frustration. "Haul ass. They're going to keep this up until you do."

Felix edged past Jamie, the dogs lunging and snapping at his heels. His legs trembled. He stripped off his clothes, tossing his shirt and pants outside the bathroom, and climbed into the shower.

After he was clean, after he had calmed down, he pulled his bathrobe around him and ventured out.

Jamie had cleared his clothes away from the hallway. He had also put the dogs outside, Felix was relieved to note. Jamie sat on the couch in the dark living room, smoking a joint. It was the first time Felix had ever seen him smoke inside the building.

He looked up at Felix and didn't say anything. Felix perched on the leather easy chair across from him, carefully arranging his short robe around his knees.

Jamie's hand shook a little as he brought the joint to his lips. He took a long drag, then looked over at Felix. "Somebody has been doing something he shouldn't," he said. "Where were you?"

Felix stared at him for a minute. Jamie sounded mad, or scared, or some mixture of the two. "I was out. With Tasha, from work," he said.

"Where were you, and what were you doing?" Jamie asked.

Felix felt his face grow hot from some combination of confusion and embarrassment. "I don't know why it's your business."

Jamie smoked in silence. "Maybe it's not. But it might be a good idea to let me in on whatever's going on," he said. His tone was calmer now.

He passed him the joint. Felix shook his head. "You sure? Might help. You look like you're on the verge of collapse."

"I'm okay," Felix said. "I mean, I'm not okay, but . . ."

He trailed off. Jamie observed him. "So, the lock. Let's start there."

"Yeah. I meant to get that fixed today." Felix exhaled. "Nicky and Claire broke in last night. They're looking for Michael."

"That's where you got the bruises?" Jamie gestured toward his forehead.

Felix nodded. "Nicky beat me up. And then he burned me." He spread the collar of his robe to show Jamie the fresh gauze patch.

"With his hand, like the way you said Claire did earlier?"

"Yeah." Felix felt crumpled, fatigued. "They killed Chad, that intern at my company. Nicky did, at least. And I'm pretty sure he killed some other kid last night after leaving here." His vision blurred. "I couldn't get a hold of Michael, so I don't know if he's okay. And things are weird at my workplace, and I don't understand anything." He searched around for words, then gave up. "I'm just so tired."

"Okay, Felix." Jamie's voice was calm. "Michael's fine. He's safe on a bus somewhere. Don't worry about him right now."

"I told them, though." He couldn't feel any more miserable. "Nicky and Claire. I told them Michael was going back to Chicago. They might follow him there."

"Are you beating yourself up about that?"

"Yeah." Felix swallowed. "I'm his brother. I should protect him better than that."

"They hurt you." The pale blue eyes were even more intense than usual. "They ambushed you, and they hurt you. Cut yourself some slack and move on. You can't do much for Michael right now, so let's focus on keeping you out of further trouble. Where were you tonight?"

"At work. Atomic."

"This late?"

Felix shook his head. "Nicky showed up at this party at the company founder's house last night. Loudon Strong, he seems nice but he's maybe kind of weird. Anyway, Tasha and I went to see if he knew anything about Nicky."

"And?"

"He said he didn't."

"But you don't believe him." Jamie examined him. "When you say he's 'weird', what do you mean?"

"I'm not even sure I could explain," Felix said. "Just that a lot's been happening lately that I don't understand."

"Welcome to Los Angeles." Jamie managed a low-wattage grin. "The ladies smelled something on you, Felix. Something bad. Maybe something evil."

There had been something in Loudon's office tonight—
"evil" was too strong a word, but something in that general
direction. "What do you mean?"

Jamie shrugged. "There's evil in this city, pockets of it here
and there. Sounds like you maybe stumbled into the fringes of it
tonight."

He was quiet for a minute. "Stay away from them as much
as you can. Tasha and Loudon Strong," he said at last.

"Makes sense." Felix got to his feet. He felt like his body
was made out of something heavy and inflexible. Soggy bags of
sand, maybe. "I just want to go to bed now."

"Sure. Get some sleep. I'll keep Gretchen and Heidi inside
tonight," Jamie said. "If anyone tries to break in, they'll let us
know."

"Good idea." Felix staggered off in the direction of his
room.

"It's probably going to be okay, Felix," Jamie called after
him.

Under the circumstances, that wasn't terribly reassuring.

CHAPTER THIRTEEN

ON TELEVISION, RIDPATH Washburn looked brooding and dangerous: thick neck, muscular upper body, shaved head, a savage beak of a nose. In person, he was petite and gregarious. He'd already given Felix a chatty, anecdote-laden tour of the downtown set of his hit series, *Anathema*, before guiding him to a quiet corner where they could sit down for an interview. They were joined by one of *The Big Boom's* camera operators, Vanessa, who fixed her digital camera up on a tripod and checked her phone restlessly while they chatted.

In Ridpath's agreeable company, the weirdness of the past few days faded more and more into the realm of the unreal. Felix's burn was healing; his bruises were fading. At some point, Nicky and Claire would be a distant memory.

"I really like the show," Felix said. "It's different than what I thought it'd be. I thought it was just a crime drama, and then the whole supernatural element took me by surprise, when it started turning out that you're all magical creatures or whatever. It blew my mind."

Ridpath grinned. "You and a lot of viewers, Felix." Felix would never get over the faint thrill that came from having celebrities smile at him and address him by name. "When I got the first script, man, I was just blown away by all the twists. We have some amazing writers. I love the direction they're taking Carlos."

That would be Carlos Mater, Ridpath's character. The press kit for *Anathema* summarized Carlos as ". . . *the handsome and dangerous head of a shadowy cabal of powerful criminals who head up Los Angeles' supernatural underbelly.*" Before heading for his set visit, Felix had looked up the definition of "cabal". And of "anathema".

"So what's going to happen this season? Are we going to find out Carlos's deal?" Felix asked. "Is he going to turn out to be a sorcerer, or a demon, or what?"

Ridpath laughed. "The writers don't tell me that kind of thing, probably because they know I'd tell you all about it. I'm not sure it's the kind of thing we're ever going to find out. Maybe even they don't know."

He glanced up and called across the stage. "Hey! Charlotte! You want to come over and talk to my man Felix from *The Big Boom*?"

Charlotte Dent, Ridpath's co-star, a petite blonde actress whom Felix thought he remembered seeing in some late night cable movie or other, strolled over. "Hi, Ridpath. Nice to meet you, Felix. I don't want to interrupt your interview."

Charlotte played Penny, the slinky, lethal henchwoman to Ridpath's sinister and enigmatic business mogul. On the screen, she was formidable, all stylish suits paired with cold stares; in person, dressed in a hoodie over yoga pants, no makeup on her scrubbed face, she seemed friendly and approachable.

Ridpath grinned up at her. "Sit down and join us for a second. You can tell Felix here about how awesome I am."

"Lies, all of it," Charlotte said. "We despise each other." She sank into an empty chair and reached over to pat Ridpath's knee.

This was an easy interview. Charlotte and Ridpath had a natural chemistry together, gentle ribbing interspersed with compliments, and conversation flowed smoothly. After a few minutes, Charlotte excused herself with a kiss to Ridpath and a firm handshake with Felix and left them to continue their chat. Felix didn't even need to refer to his list of questions on his tablet; the interview unfurled as a seamless dialogue about the show's breakthrough first season, about its critical and commercial success, about Ridpath's Emmy nomination.

Ridpath rose from his seat. "You want to walk around outside a bit? Get some fresh air?"

"Sure." Felix fell into step with him. Vanessa shouldered her camera and trailed them out of the gorgeous old Art Deco building that served as Carlos Mater's lair.

This was a section of downtown that had recently been significantly upgraded—gentrified, Felix supposed the term was—though it still bordered one of the sketchier areas of the city. The film trucks were set up on Main Street along the western border of Skid Row. On the opposite side of the street, the neighborhood took a dive. No more refurbished lofts and upscale condominiums; instead, Felix saw boarded-up buildings and fenced-off parking lots. People shuffled by, many wrapped in bulky garments despite the afternoon heat. A young bald woman in a t-shirt and no pants shouted something incomprehensible over and over, her small body trembling with unrestrained anger.

Ridpath gestured at the woman. "Mental illness. She's out here all the time. There are a lot of people like her around here." His thick brows drew together. "We film in this area a couple days a week, usually. We set up our trailers and our trucks and our craft services smack in the middle of Skid Row. It's their neighborhood, and it's hard not to feel like a hostile intruder sometimes."

"Is it dangerous?" Felix asked.

Ridpath shrugged. "Not for us. If you live here, yeah, it's probably not an easy life. The production tries to help a little. Leftover food gets donated to one of the missions at the end of the day, and they sometimes hire the locals as extras. We try to be as benign as we can. In the end, though, I'm never sure if the good is balancing the harm."

He stared at the ranting woman for a moment longer, shaking his head. He turned to Felix and grinned again. "Sorry. That was my moment of actorly self-seriousness for the day," he said. "This is a damn good show, and a great opportunity for me. Hell, this is freaking Shakespeare, compared to what I was doing before this."

"*Interstellar Boys?*"

Ridpath nodded. "Yeah. You ever see that hot mess? Started out pretty promising, actually, I have to keep reminding myself that the early seasons didn't always suck ass, but man, *that* was a train wreck of increasingly hilarious proportions." He shrugged. "Still, though, I'd never have this job if it wasn't for that. And I met some nice people there."

He threw Felix a surprisingly sly look. "I keep in touch with my girl Kelsey Kirkpatrick. Hell of a sweet kid."

Kelsey Kirkpatrick. Seemed like a lifetime ago. "I interviewed her last week for the *Cold Inferno* junket."

"I know that, brother. I saw that. It's why I'm mentioning it. Thanks for not bringing up the obvious with her. You're a class act, Felix."

"I don't know if it's class so much as . . . I don't know. Cowardice, probably. I got in trouble with our executive producer for dropping the ball. The general consensus seems to be that Kelsey wanted to talk about the tape, and I messed up by not mentioning it. I guess I chickened out."

"It's called having a sense of decorum, Felix. Which isn't the sort of thing that'll help you much as an entertainment reporter, but it makes you a decent human being in my book."

Felix paused, wondering how to raise the issue without causing offense. "There seem to be a lot of people who think she leaked the tape herself for the publicity."

"Sure. It's possible. She wouldn't be the first, and it wouldn't be that much out of character. I love Kelsey, but she's still just a kid, and kids do dumb things. But look, either her version of the story is true and you'd be asking her some very public questions about a very bad violation of her privacy, or you'd be enabling her bid for attention. Either way, you shouldn't beat yourself up for chickening out, as you put it." Ridpath grinned at him again. "You need anything else from me? They're going to be ready for me on the set soon."

"No, that's everything. Thanks for talking to me."

"No problem." Ridpath shook his hand and simultaneously clapped him on the back as though they were old friends, then sauntered back inside the building.

Vanessa lowered her camera. "We're good?" she asked Felix.

"Yeah. I think that's it," he said. "Hey, are you heading straight to Atomic from here?"

She shook her head. "I'm in Burbank after this. Tasha needs me at Warner. Why?"

"I was hoping to grab a ride. My car broke down yesterday. I took a taxi here."

Vanessa looked at him like he was crazy. "Why didn't you get a rental?"

His credit card had been declined by the car rental site. "A taxi seemed like less hassle at the time," he said. "I'll call another taxi. It's no problem."

"Well, it's not *my* problem, at least," Vanessa said cheerfully. "Take the subway, if you're feeling adventurous. I think it stops somewhere around here."

Felix stared at her. "L.A. has a subway?"

"I have no first-hand experience, but that's the rumor." She bundled her tripod under her arm and threw Felix a wave over her shoulder, then headed off in the direction of the parking structure.

And here Felix was, all alone on Skid Row. Hailing taxis on the streets in Los Angeles was an impossibility, even in good neighborhoods. He took out his phone to order a cab.

Another scream from the pantless bald woman caught his attention. He glanced across the street.

Ah. That wasn't good. The woman from the Atomic courtyard yesterday, the one-armed Asian woman with the bleached hair and the damaged eye, she was there, sitting on the sidewalk, knees pulled to her chest, leaning her back against the wall. Her head was down, but she was right across the street from him, and it was definitely her, and it was far too much of a coincidence to ignore.

Felix started walking. Very calmly, striding purposefully away from Skid Row, heading in the direction of all the nice shiny skyscrapers peeking over the top of Bunker Hill. He didn't know the area too well, but skyscrapers meant big shops and nice restaurants and people in expensive business suits, and that seemed safer right now.

He reached Pershing Square, a small paved park. Well, damn—Vanessa was right. There it was, a wide glass canopy marking the entrance to the subway. He paused, indecisive.

He could wait here for a taxi. He could keep walking until he reached a safer area. Or he could hop on the subway.

The urge to get out of this neighborhood as quickly as possible came over him. He descended a long escalator into the bowels of the city.

The station was airy and clean and simple to navigate: The train in one direction would take him to Hollywood, and the train in the other direction would take him deeper into downtown. He'd taken the train in New York often enough, and the comparative simplicity of this one was almost jarring.

There she was, the one-armed woman. She used a cane, he noticed for the first time, though it hadn't seemed to slow her down much, since she'd kept pace with him for several blocks. A slight hitch to her walk, that was all. She strode past him without looking at him, then leaned against the wall further down on the platform, her cane clutched in her sole hand.

It seemed like she was making a concerted effort not to look at him. She was trailing him, she absolutely had to be trailing him, and while it was hard to connect her with Nicky and Claire, it was also hard to think she *wouldn't* be related to the recent violent strangeness in his life.

The train arrived. A fast decision—get on it, or leave now and try to lose the woman? Felix stepped on board. The woman entered the next car down.

If he got off at Western, he'd be fairly close to Atomic, but he'd be out in the open, exposed and unprotected. He stayed on the train a few stops further, then joined the small crowd exiting at Highland, right at the base of the shopping complex and the big theater where they held the Academy Awards. This was a familiar neighborhood to Felix, and while it probably wasn't much safer than downtown, it was more comfortable.

The surface was heat and chaos, Hollywood Boulevard in all its mad, grimy glory. The escalator spat him up into a horde of tourists and panhandlers.

First priority was to lose his tail. He walked across the pink stars emblazoned with gold names on the dirty sidewalk and sped up the stairs leading into the open-air shopping center, which featured multiple levels of shops and restaurants surrounding an open atrium. He knew the layout; he could shake his stalker here.

Shaky from adrenaline, he headed all the way to the top level and found a small table nestled in an alcove. He could look down at the atrium from here, but he'd be hard to spot. He sat and felt his pulse return to normal.

There she was, her trench coat too heavy for a hot summer day, the right sleeve still pinned to the shoulder over her missing arm. She stood at the railing of the second level, her mouth drawn in a grim line.

Three times wasn't a coincidence. What was the saying? It was enemy action. She was following him. Why? That she was a fan seemed unlikely. It also seemed unlikely she was an associate of Claire and Nicky's—her ragged appearance was too much of a contrast to their polished sleekness—but she was following him, like they had followed him, and they had ended up hurting him.

He shrank back into the alcove, hunching down and watching her as she looked out over the atrium. Looking for him.

After a while, she turned and left. Felix remained where he was for a very long time.

CHAPTER FOURTEEN

THE JUICE BAR at Pumped! was too bright and too busy to encourage lingering, but Felix was exhausted, and he wanted to linger. He'd made it through only half of his workout—his trainer, Jurgen, had yelled something at him about slackers and quitters, but for once he was too miserable to let verbal abuse spur him on to greater effort. Now he was sipping liquefied amaranth leaves mixed with lemon juice and cayenne while trying to summon up the energy to drive home.

On the counter beside him, his phone chirped once. He glanced down at the display screen.

He picked it up. "Michael?"

A pause, then his brother's voice came over the line, distant and thin. "I got your message."

Michael sounded exhausted, too. "Are you back in Chicago?"

"Yeah. I made it in a while ago. Sorry for not getting back to you earlier; I had my phone turned off for most of the trip." Michael paused again. "In your voicemail, you said I might be in danger."

"Yeah." Felix glanced around and lowered his voice. The place was crowded and the noise level was high, and no one was paying him any attention, but even still, it would've been better to field this call at home. "People are looking for you. You know that, right?"

"Nicky and Claire." The weary resignation in Michael's tone alarmed Felix. "You said they talked to you?"

"A couple of times, yeah. What do they want with you?"

"It doesn't matter," Michael said. "Do you know what they can do?"

"I know they burn things. Is that what you mean?"

Michael was quiet. Then: "Do you believe me now, that I didn't start those fires?"

There was almost a decade of hurt and resentment in those words. "It was them all along, wasn't it?"

"I guess you've figured out . . . they're not human. You know they're not human, right?"

"What are they, Michael?" Felix tried to keep his voice steady.

"They're made of fire, that's all I really know. When I was a kid, I thought they lived inside me, but that's not it. I don't know if they're from another dimension or what, but they use my body whenever they want to travel from there to here. They pass through me and emerge out of my chest."

"Wouldn't that kill you?" Felix asked.

"You'd think so, wouldn't you?" On the other end of the line, Michael made a noise that sounded like a snort. "I don't know why it doesn't. It hurts like hell while it's happening, but I seem to recover from it pretty quickly."

"They can change their appearance, can't they?" Felix asked.

"When they first come out of me, they don't even look like people. They're kind of like black flames in a blobby shape. And then they start shifting into human form."

"Did they find you in Chicago? Is that why you came to visit me?"

"Yeah." Michael sounded weary and resigned. "I didn't think they'd track me to L.A. so quickly."

"They beat you here," Felix said. "By a couple of days. How'd they know where you were going?"

"You're my big brother, and I was in trouble. Where else was I going to go?"

Felix felt his chest tighten at that. "I told them you got on a bus back to Chicago," he said. "I'm sorry. I didn't know what else to tell them."

He heard Michael exhale deeply on the other end of the line. "Did they hurt you?" he asked.

"No. They just scared me. I'm fine."

Michael fell silent. "I'm sorry I got you involved in this," he said at last.

"Michael . . ." There was a click, and Felix was talking to a dead line.

He replaced the phone on the table. He felt more exhausted than before, broken and helpless.

You know they're not human, right?

He jumped at a hand on his shoulder, almost knocking over his amaranth juice. A dark-haired woman, a stranger, looked at him with a startled expression.

"Sorry! Didn't mean to sneak up on you." She smiled. "Felix, right? I'm Shelley. We met last week at Coal? Your roommate's band was playing?"

Shelley. That was right. The woman he'd chatted with before Claire's arrival.

"Of course. Hi," he said. "Is this your gym?"

She wasn't dressed for the gym. She was dressed in a green silk blouse and skinny jeans with gold wedge heels. She looked very, very good. She shook her head. "I saw you through the window. I was dropping off my dry cleaning next door." She paused. "Is everything okay? Not to pry, but you look upset."

"Rough workout." He managed a smile. "Do you want to sit down? I can get you a juice or something."

She looked at the clumpy green sludge in his glass and wrinkled her nose. "I'll pass, thanks." She cleared her throat. "Look, I was just going to see about maybe finding some dinner somewhere. Maybe you could join me?"

He hadn't really clicked with Shelley at Coal. He barely remembered their conversation, but she'd been dismissive about the Midwest, and he'd felt defensive. She looked friendlier now— a little apologetic, full of concern for him—and she was gorgeous, and maybe he just needed a relaxing dinner out with a beautiful woman, where he didn't have to think about Nicky or Claire or Michael or Loudon Strong.

Maybe he just needed to eat.

"I'd like that," he said.

They ended up at a Mexican restaurant on Fountain, someplace small and dark and intimate. Felix sipped a margarita the size of a bowling ball and split a monstrous lobster nacho platter with Shelley. Shelley liked to eat, which was rare among women—rare among people—in Los Angeles.

She also liked to listen. She didn't want to talk about her PR job, and Felix could respect that; maybe she didn't want him to milk her for her industry connections. She asked about Atomic, about his ongoing competition with Jenny, about his future goals. They ate, and talked, and drank. He felt warm and wobbly after the first gigantic margarita. When she tried to press a second round on him, his first instinct was to pass.

"Live it up," she said. "I'm driving you home anyway." Felix's car was still in the shop until tomorrow; he'd taken a taxi to the gym straight from work. There'd been no further sightings of the mysterious one-armed Asian woman, though he'd been constantly on the alert.

Felix hesitated, then nodded at their waiter. He'd probably regret it later, but it was lovely sitting here with Shelley, just talking and eating and forgetting about the awfulness in his life.

"Everything okay with you?" Shelley asked. "I don't want to be intrusive, but you seem sad."

"It's fine," Felix said. "I'm having a few family problems right now."

"Anything you want to talk about?"

He did want to talk about it, sort of, but "my brother is being hunted by a pair of murderous fire creatures" was a conversation killer, so he shook his head. "It's no big deal."

She stared at him, resting her chin in her hands. Her eyes were very dark and wide. "You want to get out of here?" she asked. "We can go somewhere quiet."

It was pretty quiet in the restaurant, but that clearly wasn't what Shelley meant. After a bit of discussion, they ended up driving into the hills. Felix hadn't wanted to go back to his place, because it was always possible Nicky and Claire would be there waiting for him, and Shelley lived all the way at the beach, so they went up to Mulholland and parked on the edge of the bluff overlooking the entire city. Shelley drove a dusty pickup truck, incongruous with her Angeleno sleekness. Were they going to make out in the front, like teenagers? The thought vanished when

Shelley slipped out of the driver's seat and gestured for him to follow her. "I want to show you this."

It was dark up here, the blanket of city lights starting at the base of the hill and covering the land as far as he could see in all directions. Felix followed her along the edge of the bluff. "Where are we going?"

"I found this place while hiking. It's kind of neat." She slipped through the gap between two concrete safety barriers and headed down the hill on a well-worn dirt pathway that wove in between the trees and shrubs. Her wedge heels were entirely the wrong footwear for this terrain. Felix had changed back into his street clothes after his workout, and his loafers didn't have much traction on the crumbling hillside, either.

He hesitated, thinking of rattlesnakes and coyotes. "Is this safe?"

"Sure. It's not far. Come on." The night air was warm. The air smelled like sagebrush and smoke.

She led the way down the path to a small open shack made of pine logs. "Take a seat. We can have some privacy, and you can't beat the view."

The split logs that formed the steps were dirty, but Felix couldn't see any snakes or other obvious dangers around, so he sat beside her, facing the city skyline. "Just look at that view and try to relax a little," she said.

He cleared his throat. "It's nice," he said.

This was the kind of situation where he should make a move. Clearly, some kind of move was warranted. While he was considering this, Shelley nestled closer to him. Her hand slipped around his back and rested on his hip.

There was something a little possessive about her grip on him. Her slim hand moved around to the back of his neck and applied gentle pressure, pulling him toward her. Felix leaned over.

She knew how to kiss. Her mouth ravaged his, her tongue showing no hesitation in exploiting his mouth. Felix's knees got a little weak for a moment.

She pulled back and looked at him. She raked her teeth across her bottom lip, as if tasting the remnants of him. "It's too warm for that shirt," she said.

Felix agreed. The light, loose weave had been cool against his skin when he put it on this morning, but it was made from some synthetic blend that didn't breathe well, and now it felt damp and scratchy. Shelley reached for the hem and pulled it over his head in one clean movement, then tossed it to the side.

She looked at the gauze patch taped over his burn. "What's that?"

"I had a tattoo removed." It was the first thought that sprang into his brain. The side of Shelley's mouth tugged, like she was thinking he wasn't the type for tattoos, but she said nothing.

He leaned in and kissed her again, hands sliding up her back. He wished he knew how to whisk her shirt off with the same panache she'd demonstrated with his. It had a loose, draping neckline, and there was little chance he could yank it over her head without tangling it in her hoop earrings. He settled for slipping his hands under her shirt and moving his hands up her bare skin.

Her mouth left his and trailed down his chin, his neck. "You're lovely, Felix," she murmured against his skin. "I thought that when I first saw you at the club, you were so beautiful and fragile."

Fragile? Was that really a compliment? Before he could reply, she leaned back against the dusty wood floor of the shack and pulled him down on top of her. As her lips returned to his, her hands moved to the front of his jeans, which he figured gave him permission to slide his hands around to the front of her body. He slipped his hands into the microfiber cups of her bra, ever vigilant for any sign of disapproval on her part.

His pants were unbuttoned. Her hands were down his pants. So unfair that she still somehow had all her clothes on. Giving up on her shirt for the moment, he moved his hands to the low waistband of her jeans. His hand ducked under the thin elastic strap of her thong underwear and came to rest on her hipbone.

Something was strange with her skin here. It wasn't dry and smooth like the rest of her. It felt rubbery under his fingertips, almost sticky. It wasn't skin at all. It couldn't be. It was too warm, and it grew warmer the longer he touched it.

She made a small noise of surprise, then pulled one of her hands out of the front of his pants and placed it over his. She moved his hand away from her hip. "No, it's okay," she said as he drew back and looked at her in mounting shock. "Don't worry about it. Let's just keep going."

"But what——?" He trailed off. Her dark hair seemed to be absorbing the color of the pine floor. Even as Felix watched, it lightened and faded to a pale blonde. Her bare skin under Felix's hands moved, pulsated, like something was swimming beneath the surface of her flesh. Her skin was stretching, changing shape, growing warmer and warmer.

In the dim light, she glowed.

Felix recoiled. "What's going on?"

"It's okay, darling, it's okay," Shelley said. She placed a comforting hand on his neck. Only now she was Claire, not Shelley.

"I didn't mean to scare you. I can't hold onto one shape for long. I have to keep adjusting."

Felix shot to his feet. She rose as well. "I need you to stay calm, Felix."

"What did you do with Shelley?" he asked. His voice was high and breathless.

"Nothing. I don't even know her. I tried my best to look like her, because I knew you were attracted to her at the club, and I knew you were scared of me."

"Because you tortured me!" Felix said.

"I know. But that was mostly Nicky, and Nicky doesn't know I'm here." She touched his cheek. Hot to the touch. Felix flinched away. "I thought this might give us a chance to talk about Michael without Nicky getting in the way."

"What do you want with Michael? What do you need him for?"

"Well, see, that's not really what I meant," she said. She smiled. "I meant you could do the talking. Tell me where you're hiding him, and I'll tell Nicky, and he and I will leave you alone forever." She shrugged. "Because otherwise, Nicky is going to come after you again, and this time I won't be able to talk him out of doing some serious damage to you."

"He's in Chicago. I told you the truth earlier, Michael's back in Chicago. He called me today at the gym, right before you found me."

"He's still here." Her voice was harsh. "He's still in this city. I can almost see him. When I close my eyes, he's like a glowing ball dancing at the edges of my vision. I'd know if he left."

"I don't know anything about that," Felix said. "He called me, I promise he called me, and said he was in Chicago. That's all I know. You need to believe me."

She stared at him, her expression solemn. "No," she said slowly. "I think you're going to have to do more to convince me, darling."

She grabbed his wrist. Her fingers burned, the pain bright and immediate. He yanked back as hard as he could.

The skin across her elbow, right under the sleeve of her shirt, stretched and *tore* as he pulled. Her sleeve caught on fire. She made a noise, a high yelp of pain, and let go of Felix.

The flames rushed up her sleeve and ignited her hair before Felix had sorted out what was happening. Her skin wasn't burning. It was falling in on itself, melting, changing texture.

Claire shrieked and swatted at the flames. "Put them out, put them out!"

Felix stared at her, immobile. She screeched, a long high note of panicked agony.

He couldn't stand to see anyone in that much pain. He scooped up his abandoned shirt and tried to smother the flames. Her melting skin stuck to the fabric in viscous threads, like she was made of rubber cement.

She howled again, the flames consuming her hair, her blouse, her jeans. It was too hot to stay near her anymore. Felix backed up out of the reach of the flames.

She was a creature of flame and destruction, something un-earthly and terrifying, and now she was dying. As soon as the flames consumed her clothes, she melted, while Felix watched in numb horror. When it was over, only a charred pile of jewelry remained on a glistening pool of what looked like flesh-colored melted rubber.

He almost couldn't make it out of the shed before vomiting, the margaritas and nachos working their way up and out of his system with vigorous force.

Someone might have seen the flames, or heard Claire's shouts. Not that it mattered; anyone arriving on the scene would just find Felix, sick and drunk and alone. Even still, he forced himself to straighten up and button his pants. His shirt was beyond repair, so he left it behind with the paltry traces of what had once been Claire, and climbed back up the hill to Mulholland.

His wrist was burned. He was shirtless and stranded— maybe if he poked around the melted puddle that used to be Claire, he'd find the keys to her truck, but the truck was almost certainly stolen, so that sounded like a bad idea.

He called Jamie. Jamie picked up on the first ring. "Felix? What's wrong?"

Felix paused. "How'd you know something's wrong?" he asked.

"Because trouble is finding you all over the place these days. What's going on?"

"Are you in the middle of something? Can you pick me up?" he asked.

"Band practice, but I can leave if it's an emergency."

"It is, kind of." Felix exhaled and looked around. Everything was quiet and still, but he couldn't stand being out here, alone and scared and sick. "I'm stranded up on Mulholland." He gave the best directions he could. "Can you get here fast? Something scary happened, and I don't know if I'm still in danger."

"Fifteen minutes," Jamie said, and clicked off.

Almost as soon as Jamie disconnected the call, the phone rang again. Felix stared at the unfamiliar number, tempted to ignore it. "Hello?"

"Felix Dockweiler?" A woman's voice, unfamiliar.

"Who's this?"

"This is Poppy Kang from Sparky Mother's office." None of those names meant anything to him, but the woman—Poppy—continued smoothly without giving him a chance to speak. "You recently visited Loudon Strong about a certain matter?"

He was silent. Poppy paused, then resumed speaking once it became apparent he wasn't going to reply. "Sparky was wondering if you'd stop by his office tomorrow. He thinks you might be able to help each other out."

"Wait. I'm sorry. Who's Sparky Mother?" Was he getting the name right? That couldn't be right, could it?

Poppy sounded amused. "All you need to know right now is that Loudon Strong answers to Sparky. Should we say noon tomorrow?"

"I can't. I have to work. I won't be able to—"

"Take a long lunch," Poppy said. Yes, that was definitely amusement in her voice, and something about that made Felix relax a little. Poppy sounded good-natured and friendly. "Trust me, you'll want to make this meeting. We're in Koreatown. It's not all that far from Atomic, and it shouldn't take too much out of your day."

"I suppose that's okay," Felix said. "Listen, can you just tell me what—?"

"Excellent. Tomorrow at noon. I'll email you the directions." Poppy hung up before Felix could ask any more questions, or even give her his email address.

He stared at the phone, confused and worried.

CHAPTER FIFTEEN

SPARKY MOTHER'S OFFICE was located on a shabby stretch of Wilshire west of downtown's posh financial district. The building didn't have a parking structure, so Felix parked his freshly-repaired car on a side street in front of a closed Korean karaoke bar. A trio of pretty Asian teens passed him on the sidewalk, teetering on high platform boots paired with satin track shorts, swinging purses shaped like cartoon animals and drinking bubble tea through chunky neon straws.

Felix frowned and double-checked the address Poppy Kang had emailed him. Sparky's office building seemed to be abandoned. It had no identifying features, no signs indicating what businesses were housed within. It was a teetering structure of steel and smoky glass, but the front windows of the ground floor were cloudy, as if they had been soaped over from the inside. The outside stairs were strewn with old newspapers and fast-food wrappers. The building was surrounded by a rusty chain-link fence, the front gate propped open with a cinder block.

"Hey, supermodel." A man in a dirty white t-shirt sat cross-legged on an unfolded cardboard box on the sidewalk in front of the fence. He beckoned Felix over to him.

The man grinned up at him. All of his lower front teeth were missing. He wore a baseball cap fastened to his head with a kerchief knotted beneath his chin. Patches of brown skin across his nose had peeled off, exposing shiny pinkish-white skin beneath.

A tiny black cat perched on his shoulders. As Felix approached, the cat hopped up to the top of the man's head and glowered at him. The man squinted up at Felix under the bill of his cap, seemingly unaware of the cat on his head. "You look a little lost, supermodel."

Felix gestured at the building. "I have an appointment in there, but I'm wondering if I have the right place. It looks deserted."

The man glanced over his shoulder. His lips came together in a thin line. "It ain't exactly deserted, but it ain't your kind of place either. Who's your business with?"

"I'm supposed to see someone named Sparky Mother." The name still didn't sound right, no matter how many times he said it.

The cat yawned, baring tiny pointed teeth, then jumped off the man's head and curled up beside him on the cardboard. The man grunted. "Eh. Sparky. Yeah, Sparky's in there, all right." He scratched the cat behind the ears with two stubby fingers.

"You know him?" Felix asked.

Another grunt. "Know of him, you could say. Man's reputation precedes him."

"Then maybe you could tell me—what kind of business is he in?"

The man looked up at him from the sidewalk. There was resignation and weariness in his expression. "Couldn't say. But you'd best be careful. Sparky Mother eats pretty kids like you for lunch."

"Real nice, Julio." A woman slipped through the open gate and approached them. She was Asian, with bobbed copper hair that shone in the bright sun. She wore a dark green skirted suit over a bronze satin blouse with a high mandarin collar paired with teetering black stilettos. "Don't scare off our visitors. It's not polite."

She smiled at Felix and extended her hand. "You must be Felix. I'm Poppy. We spoke on the phone." She had on a great deal of makeup, expertly applied, with glossy rose lips and thick, dark eyelashes. She looked like an expensive porcelain doll, decorative and far too pristine for the shabby surroundings.

"Of course. Hi," Felix said. He shook her hand. "I wasn't sure I had the right place."

The smile widened. "I figured as much. I thought it might be a good idea to try to meet you outside." She turned to the homeless man. "Thanks for looking after Felix, Julio."

"Happy to be of service, sister," Julio said. "Cute little thing like Felix here, though, I have to wonder what you and your big bad boss want with him."

"Here." Poppy held out something to Julio, a twenty folded into thirds. She wasn't carrying a purse, and her suit didn't have pockets, so she must've been palming it the entire time. "Get yourself some lunch. When your blood sugar gets low, you get a little reckless."

Julio shook his head. "Keep your money, sister. No disrespect meant to you or your boss, but I don't want to be owing you any favors." He considered. "Though I'd take spare change, if you've got any quarters on you. Think I need to make a phone call."

Poppy tilted her head to the side and examined him, bemused curiosity on her beautiful face. "Now, who might you be

123

calling, I wonder?" She nodded at him. "Try to stay out of mischief, Julio. Felix, you want to come with me?"

Felix hesitated. Julio gave him a nod. "Go ahead, Felix, I was just teasing you. Poppy here will take good care of you."

Poppy smiled at him, radiating good humor and basic human niceness. "Come on."

Reassured by that smile, Felix followed her up the dirty steps and through the glass front door, which had been smashed into a spiderweb of tiny cracks. The overhead lights in the lobby were off. Exposed floorboards sagged under his feet. To the right was the open entrance to a vacant and abandoned cocktail lounge, a banner in Korean advertising Hite beer sagging on the wall above the dusty bar.

He trailed Poppy into the elevator, which was open and waiting. She pressed the button for the penthouse level. The doors slid closed, plunging them into complete darkness.

Felix felt a surge of panic. "Is the power out?"

"This is normal," Poppy said. He couldn't see her, but she sounded amused. "Things are a bit rustic around here. I know it's a little disconcerting at first."

The elevator lurched to life. There was neither light nor sound, no comforting hum of electricity. It rose smoothly and silently until it came to a halt with another lurch. The doors slid open.

The penthouse level, like the lobby, looked unfinished. Exposed metal ducts crisscrossed the ceiling in all directions. Plywood boards spread with sheets of plastic covered the floor.

There was a reception area just to the right of the elevators. The woman at the high counter looked up at Felix as they approached. She was thin, her face brittle and bony under a heavy layer of makeup. A wireless headset extended along her jawline in

124

a slash of metal and black plastic leading from her ear to her mouth.

Poppy nodded at her. "Rachel, can you let Sparky know Felix is here?"

Rachel smiled, red lips pulling back almost to her ears. Her long teeth were so white they looked blue. "Sure thing, Poppy."

"Have a seat, Felix. Sparky will be with you in a bit," Poppy told him. She patted him on the arm and turned away.

"You're not staying?" Felix asked. It sounded a little panicky.

Poppy glanced back at him, her expression sympathetic. "Did Julio's comments make you feel a little iffy about this?"

"Sort of. Mostly I'm just confused about why I'm here."

"It happens a lot." Another nice smile. "Don't worry about anything. You and Sparky will get along just fine." She patted his arm again, her touch light and comforting, before disappearing through a set of doors at the other end of the bank of elevators.

Rachel smiled at him again. Felix wished she wouldn't. Her smile was downright creepy.

The reception area didn't fit with what Felix had seen of the building thus far. The chairs were overstuffed cubes of cushiony cobalt suede; the coffee table was a knifelike triangle of violet acrylic on a narrow chrome base. He perched on one of the cubes and tried to relax.

He didn't have long to wait before another young woman approached him. "Mr. Dockweiler? Come with me, please."

She was very tall, maybe six feet, and she was even thinner than the receptionist, almost emaciated. Felix followed her. She had the same brittle appearance as the receptionist, with the same wireless headset and a mass of tight dark curls held away from her face in a high, severe ponytail. She teetered on six-inch heels,

125

her legs like broomsticks, as she led Felix down a plastic-covered corridor.

They approached a set of tall double doors. Before they reached them, one of the doors opened, and a young man popped his head out and glanced around. Like the receptionist, he wore a wireless headset. He grinned at the sight of Felix. "Oh, hey," he said. "Felix, right? I'm Sparky." He extended his hand. Felix caught a glimpse of a flashy gold watch beneath the French cuff of his shirt. Sparky squeezed Felix's hand once and released it. He waggled a plastic travel mug in the air. "Java break. Follow me."

The tall assistant withdrew without a word. Felix followed Sparky down another corridor and past a big room filled with a grid of unoccupied cubicles. Sparky leaned against a door with his shoulder. It swung open and revealed a standard office kitchen. Refrigerator, microwave, a cluster of round tables surrounded by plastic chairs. A framed motivational poster hung on the wall beside the vending machine, a picture of a red sunset captioned with "MAKE YOUR OWN MIRACLES".

One of the tables was piled high with ribbon-tied gift boxes and baskets overflowing with cupcakes and chocolates and bottles of wine. Sparky headed straight for the coffee maker. "Need a caffeine fix?" he asked. He waved the pot at Felix.

Felix shook his head. "I'm fine, thanks."

Sparky scooped up a generous handful of sugar cubes and dropped them into his travel mug, then poured coffee on top. He screwed the mug's plastic lid into place and shook it like a cocktail shaker.

Sparky was youngish, early thirties maybe, and he was very, very pretty. His dark hair was cut into long layers in a way that looked expensive and meticulous, like he had arrived at work straight from the salon. He had dark golden skin and beautiful eyes, midnight blue irises framed by a lot of very black lashes. He wore a soft gray suit with a royal blue shirt. Felix's own shirt was the exact same shade; Sparky glanced at him and laughed. "Hey, we're twins," he said.

Felix found himself smiling back. "Your shirt's fancier than mine," he said. "French cuffs."

"Mmm, I know. They're impractical as all hell in this day and age, but I hate passing up a chance to wear cufflinks." Sparky proffered his wrist for Felix's approval. The cufflink was fashioned in the shape of a gold scorpion, its stinger glittering with tiny rubies.

Sparky picked up a pink bakery box from the table and yanked off the satin bow. He shifted aside layers of tissue and held something between two fingers. "Check this out," he said.

It was some kind of confection, a glossy pink coating of candy molded into the shape of a mouse. "These are outstanding. Marzipan and pistachio praline dipped in white chocolate. One of my clients picks me up a box every time he visits Dresden. I get all kinds of great swag from people trying to get on my good side." He offered the box to Felix. "Go on, try one."

Felix shook his head. "They look great, but I'm not hungry."

"Live a little, Felix. If you feel too guilty about the calories, you can always barf it up later. Isn't that the routine?"

Felix stared at him. "What?"

"Sorry." Sparky smiled. His incisors were a shade too long, giving him the impression of fangs. "That was a low blow. I know you don't do that anymore. These days you just don't eat much. Which believe me, I get. Discipline. You let it slide, and next thing you know you're just some fat kid from Omaha, right?"

Felix felt the blood drain from his face. "How'd you know all that?"

"I know stuff." Sparky winked. "I like that you didn't bother denying it, by the way, even though I was being kind of a dick to you. You wouldn't believe how much of my time gets wasted by people trying to hide their secrets from me."

Before Felix could collect himself enough to come up with a reply, Sparky and his coffee mug were heading for the door. He glanced back at Felix. "You coming?"

With a quick look at the abandoned box of chocolate mice, Felix trailed Sparky out of the kitchen.

CHAPTER SIXTEEN

HE WALKED WITH Sparky back to his office. "Glad we're getting the chance to meet, Omaha. I'm going to sound like a fanboy here, but I really admire your work," Sparky said.

"Yeah?" Felix had to hurry to match step with him.

"Yeah. I was just watching that movie of yours last night on Starz, crap, what was it? I can't think of the title."

Oh. "*Frat Party USA.*"

"That's the one." Sparky grinned at him. "I've seen it four or five times by now. Phenomenal stuff."

Felix cleared his throat. "It's probably not my best work."

"I know. That's what's so fantastic about it," Sparky said. "You look like you're in pain the whole time, like the director was torturing you with hot pokers between takes to get you to perform. It's priceless."

"I don't think I looked quite that—"

"You planning on doing more films, or are you happy being a reporter?"

Sparky was connected to Loudon Strong somehow, which meant Felix should tread carefully. "I'm really happy at Atomic."

"You got the words right. Now try saying it like you believe it," Sparky said. "You know you won't ever make it, right?"

"What?"

"I phrased that wrong. Of course you don't know that. My guess is that everyone out here believes the staggering odds don't apply to them. You're probably the same. And then someday, a few years down the road, you'll realize your three-month gig on some basic-cable entertainment news show was as close to fame as you're ever going to get."

Felix stared at him. "Wow," he said. "Why do you have to say things like that?"

"I'm sure people say things like that to you all the time, Omaha. Only they're probably a little more diplomatic about it." Sparky rolled his shoulders, like he was working out a crick. "In any case, maybe the odds really don't apply to you. For one thing, you're super cute and shiny and new, and that tends to go far in this town. And for another, maybe now you've got an ace up your sleeve."

"What's that?"

"Me." Again, that charming grin. "I could do some pretty amazing things with you. But I haven't quite figured out what."

They'd reached the double doors to Sparky's office, which saved Felix from having to come up with a response. Sparky flung open both doors at once. It was a dramatic entrance to a dramatic office. Felix stopped in the doorway, stunned.

Sparky's office was neither large nor luxurious. In size and décor, it was the generic office of any mid-level executive at any large corporation. The floor-to-ceiling windows, which had no panes, were the only incongruous element. Felix stared out into open air.

Sparky walked over to his desk and plopped down in his chair with a carelessness that alarmed Felix, considering how close he was to where the floor ended, twenty stories above

Wilshire Boulevard. He gestured toward a client chair. "Take a load off, Omaha. Let's get down to business," he said.

Felix remained standing, gaping at the missing windows. Sparky nodded.

"I know," he said. "It's a little freaky at first, right? The building's in a state of transition right now. I kind of like it this way, though."

"What do you do when it rains?" Felix asked. He stepped into the room. Knees wobbled a bit. It was a relief to sink down into one of Sparky's chairs.

Sparky glanced over his shoulder. "You see any rain anywhere?" he asked.

True enough. There were no clouds of any kind in the wide expanse of sky outside the windows. It was an unbroken stretch of white haze that darkened to a dusty brown at the horizon. "I guess not. We could use it, though. It might finally do something about that," Felix said. He pointed toward the northwest, where brown plumes of smoke rose up from the still-burning Malibu fires.

"Getting a little tired of the heat and smoke?" Sparky asked.

"Well, yeah. It's been going on forever. Aren't you?" Felix asked.

Sparky shrugged. "I like hot weather. I suppose it's about time for a change, though. It'll start sometime tonight."

"What will start? Rain?" Felix asked.

Another shrug. "Sure. It'll have to be a few hours from now. Got to give the clouds some time to roll in. Of course, I'll have to stop dawdling about getting windows put up. Either that, or I'll have to move."

He winked at Felix. Felix felt reassured by the wink. It was a joke, then. Hard to get a handle on Sparky's brand of humor,

131

much of which seemed to be at Felix's expense. He cleared his throat.

"I'm still a little confused about the purpose of this meeting," he said.

Sparky grinned again. "I know. I'm sorry. And here I'm wasting your time talking about the weather. You're being a good sport about this." He looked at Felix, and his genial expression shifted into something more serious. "Monday night, you visited Loudon Strong's office. Why?"

Felix blinked. "I thought Poppy said . . . Aren't you Loudon Strong's boss?"

"In a manner of speaking. It's probably more accurate to think of me as a concerned shareholder. *Major* shareholder. Loudon hasn't said anything to me about your late night rendezvous, which I find interesting. A little bird tipped me off." Felix found himself thinking of the humorless security guard in the lobby who had checked his identification at the door. Then again, he'd first spotted the one-armed Asian woman in the courtyard right after that meeting . . .

Sparky slid his chair back from the desk, skirting dangerously close to the exposed edge of the floor. "I thought you might've been negotiating your contract with the network. I already told Loudon not to do that without checking with me first, because I haven't decided if that's the path I want to take with you. Which is why I asked for this."

He kicked something out from beneath his desk and slid it toward Felix with his Oxford-shod foot. A box. A slim, narrow file storage box, like the ones that had been in Loudon Strong's office, the ones that held contracts. The ones that made odd scratching, scuffling noises. This box looked new, and it had a freshly-printed label on it. Felix picked it up and read it: *Felix Dockweiler.*

"But you're not in there. It's empty. So if you weren't getting yourself hired, what were you doing there?"

Sparky looked serious, like Felix's answer was important to him. "I thought that was what this meeting was about," Felix said. "I was looking for my brother. He's missing, and—"

Sparky waved a hand. "No, I know that already. What I don't know is why you'd go to Loudon about it."

"Because a couple of people are after my brother, and one of them was talking to Loudon at his party, and—"

"Aha! That's it." Sparky looked satisfied, though Felix couldn't imagine why. "That's what Loudon didn't want me to know."

"I don't understand." There were so many, many things Felix didn't understand that the statement seemed grotesquely inadequate.

Sparky seemed to get his meaning. He nodded. "Don't worry about it—you did the right thing by telling me." He leaned back in his chair and slipped his hands behind his neck. He seemed lost in thought.

"Ambition," he said at last. "It can be a lovely thing. You've got plenty, but your focus is muddled. You know you want to be famous, but you're not too choosy about how you get there. Loudon's kind of the same way. But you have to know your boundaries. Know your sides." He straightened. "And in this town, you can be on my side, or you can seek power elsewhere, but you really can't do both. And I think Loudon forgot about that."

He stared at Felix without seeming to see him. Felix looked down at the cardboard box in his lap. He swallowed.

"Why do they move?" he asked.

Sparky looked up at him. "What?"

"The boxes for the contracts. Stuff moves inside them sometimes."

Sparky was expressionless for a moment, then he grinned. "So they do. Come on." He got to his feet. "Field trip."

They walked past the reception desk toward the bank of elevators. The doors to the nearest elevator slid open as Sparky approached. The elevator lights were working now, Felix noticed. Sparky hit the button for the eleventh floor.

"Where are we going?" Felix asked. Sparky grinned at him and didn't answer.

The elevator reached its destination. The doors opened. To the right was a glass door leading to what looked like an outside terrace. To the left was a padlocked metal grate.

Sparky crouched down in front of the grate and touched the lock. It slid open with an audible click. He hauled up the grate and latched it into place. He ushered Felix in front of him. "After you."

Felix stooped under the grate. Sparky followed.

They stood in a dark room lined on all sides by heavy steel shelves, each holding wire cages filled with rows of boxes. Long, flat cardboard boxes.

Sparky pulled a cage off a shelf and set it on the floor. There was a low buzz in the room, a steady rustle and murmur from the boxes. Not all the boxes, and not all the time. "These are all contracts?" Felix asked.

"Yep," Sparky said.

"There's too many just for the network," Felix said.

"Yeah. Atomic is just this cage here. I asked Loudon to send these back to me yesterday. The rest are from various companies," Sparky said. "I handle the entire entertainment industry. Agencies, production companies, networks, studios. A bunch of private individuals, too"

Felix's mouth was dry. "What do you do with them? Are you some kind of lawyer?"

Sparky laughed. It was a perfectly nice, genuine, friendly laugh. "At the risk of sounding like a walking cliché, don't you know who I am?"

Felix looked at him, looked into those pretty blue eyes, and for a moment, a sick, strange moment, he thought maybe he did know. The moment passed, and Sparky was once again just an attractive guy with an expensive haircut and a strong self-amusing streak. To distract himself from the unwanted thought that had entered into his mind, Felix looked at the box on top of the stack in the cage. He read the printed label: *Tasha Drummond.*

Something inside it rustled. A whisper, a muted thump. "What are they, really?" he asked.

He didn't know if he expected Sparky to answer. Sparky shrugged. "Take a look." He gestured at Tasha's box. "That'd be an excellent one to open, actually."

There was nothing threatening about Sparky. Nothing at all. Felix didn't know why his hands shook as he picked up the box. It was light, too light to contain files. He placed it on the cement floor and crouched beside it. He looked up at Sparky, hesitating.

"Go ahead," Sparky said.

Felix pulled at the lid. With numb fingers, he lifted it off and laid it to the side.

The box contained a single dead bird, a dirty gray-and-white feathered bird with stunted, malformed wings.

No. It wasn't a bird. It had no head, no beak, no legs, just a winged, lifeless body.

It wasn't lifeless. The bird moved. Feathers rustled, small wings stretched wide, and then something swept up and out of the box and soared toward Felix. It flew over him, or maybe it went straight through him. Along with it came a scent, or an impossibly precise memory of a scent, of basil and amber.

And then he was on his feet, backing away from the box, backing away from the scent of Tasha that was all around him, inside of him, and then the winged creature was gone. A flicker of white soared out beneath the raised grate and vanished.

Sparky replaced the lid on the empty box, then placed the box back on the shelf. He dusted off his hands on the pockets of his suit jacket and shook his head. "I'm not surprised she took off like that. She's been itching to go for a while. Though I don't know what she has to be unhappy about, the job's been everything she's ever wanted. And she's got a hell of a nice house. Four bedrooms, home theater, kidney-shaped pool in back. Pretty sweet car, too."

"That was Tasha's . . ." Felix couldn't finish.

"Contract," Sparky said. "Which you just broke." He grinned. "Just don't be too surprised if she doesn't shower you with gratitude. I think that house and that flashy little Mercedes are more important to her than she lets on."

Felix leaned against one of the shelves. The metal felt cold and substantial and reassuring against his back. He closed his eyes and inhaled. When he opened them, he saw Sparky staring at him in concern.

"You need fresh air," he said. "Come on."

Felix followed Sparky back under the metal grate. Sparky opened the door to the terrace. "Here," he said.

Felix walked to the railing and took a deep, shaky breath. The air wasn't all that fresh—it was hot and dry and smoky—but it was a relief to be away from those boxes. He looked over the railing, down at Wilshire far below.

Sparky rubbed his shoulder. "You need water or anything?" he asked.

He shook his head. "I'm okay," he said, and wondered if it was true.

Sparky leaned back against the railing. "Your brother's still in Los Angeles," he said without preamble. "I don't know where exactly, but he's pretty close. If I close my eyes, I can almost see where he's hiding. Kid's got one hell of an energy signature. Hook him up to the grid, and I bet he could power all of Koreatown."

Felix stared at him. "Why is Michael so important?"

Sparky shook his head. "It's not your brother. It's who he brings with him that's the problem." He glanced out over the horizon. "Tourists," he said finally. "On the whole, I like tourists. They're good for the economy, and they're great for perpetuating all the myths about this place. Plus they're kind of cute, what with their fanny packs and their sensible walking shoes. But the tourists hunting down your brother, they need to get out of my city. They killed those two kids."

"Chad Bryson and Timothy Quinn."

Sparky nodded. "They both fell under my jurisdiction, and it looks bad for me if I don't do anything about their deaths."

"Do you know what they are?" Felix asked. "The tourists?"

"Not specifically. Fire demons or whatever, something like that. They're strictly small-timers, but they're out of control."

"Where do they come from?" Felix asked. "Michael thought it might be another dimension."

Sparky considered this, then shrugged. "That's pretty close, actually. I don't think it'd do you any good to know the details.

There are a whole lot of different realms, and the creeps who are after your brother keep escaping from theirs."

"Why Michael?" Felix asked. "I mean, how come they can use him like that? Is it his, what'd you call it, his energy signature?"

"Don't know, exactly. It sounds like your brother might have ties to a couple of realms: here, and there. The tourists from that other realm can use him as a doorway to bop back and forth. If I had to guess, I'd say there's something a little other-than-human about your brother. How old is he, anyway?"

"He turned nineteen a few months ago."

"Great. Since there's nothing even remotely inhuman about you, unless your brother was adopted, you might want to find out what your mom was getting herself into twenty years ago."

Felix stared. "Wait. Are you really suggesting—"

Sparky winked at him. "Not to disparage your mom's character or anything, but that seems like the most likely explanation. No judgment here. Your dad was kind of an asshole, wasn't he?"

"Yeah, but how did you—?"

"Hard keeping secrets from me, remember?" Sparky looked at Felix. "I'm getting all chatty like this for your benefit, Omaha. The simplest way for me to get rid of the unwanted tourists would be to get rid of your brother. As long as he's alive, they can always come back. So I'm asking you to get your brother out of the city, okay?"

"Can you tell me where I can find him?" Felix asked.

Sparky shook his head. "My responsibility toward those two dead kids aside, I'm trying to limit my involvement in this. The fire demons, they're breaking all kinds of unwritten rules by coming here and crapping up the place, but I want to be careful about how I go about retaliating. If I can resolve this without taking direct action myself, it's better for all concerned. We all try to leave each other alone as much as we can."

"Who's 'we'?," Felix asked.

"Doesn't matter to you. Just help me settle this by getting your brother far, far away from here, and I'll be grateful. And believe me, my gratitude can be an extraordinary thing to have."

Felix opened his mouth to speak, then stopped as Sparky raised a finger for silence. Sparky tilted his head to the side, listening to something in his headset. "No. It's fine. We're on the terrace," he said in reply to a question Felix couldn't hear.

When he at last turned to Felix, there was something different in his expression. The affability and the sense that he was enjoying Felix's company were gone. The beautiful eyes narrowed. "What do you know about Young Park?" he asked.

Whatever Felix had expected him to say, it wasn't that. He stared at him. "I have no idea where that is," he said at last.

Sparky blinked, then grinned. "Omaha, you're a kick in the pants." He nodded toward the terrace door. "Watch. This will be interesting."

The glass door swung open. The one-armed Asian woman strode onto the terrace, trailed by the brittle-looking assistant with the dark curls. The assistant's features were drawn into a look of irritation that pulled her skin into tight lines around the edges.

The Asian woman stopped a few feet away from Felix and Sparky. Sparky leaned back and rested his elbows against the railing, the picture of nonchalance. "Look what crawled out of the subway," he said. "I can't imagine what business you think you have here. Felix falls under my protection, not yours."

The woman almost smiled. The damaged skin at the corner of her right eye pulled and wrinkled. "I'm dating his roommate."

"Congratulations. Felix is still mine."

"That's for him to decide." She addressed Felix. "We're leaving."

"Do you mind? We're in the middle of business," Sparky said. "Go back to Pasadena, princess, and leave us alone."

"Felix. Come on." She stepped toward him.

The assistant reached out to grab her arm. The Asian woman pivoted and struck her on the jaw with her cane.

The cane broke apart on impact. Shards of some pale material flew into the air.

No. The cane was intact. The assistant's jaw, and much of the side of her face, had shattered like smashed porcelain.

The assistant made a mew of distress and covered the dark, jagged hole in her face with her hands. There were bits of flesh-colored debris on the terrace, broken chunks of . . . skin?

The Asian woman tapped Felix on the shoulder with her cane to get his attention. "Felix," she said. "Come with me. Now."

Felix stared at her.

CHAPTER SEVENTEEN

FOR A MOMENT, there was silence. Sparky didn't move from his position against the railing. The assistant made a low keening noise. She looked up at Sparky from behind her hands, which couldn't quite cover the hole in her face.

"It's your own fault, you know," he said. "I didn't tell you to grab her." He gestured with his head toward the terrace door. "Get yourself fixed up."

The assistant shot him a venomous look and fled to the door. Sparky looked after her and shook his head. He straightened up and faced the Asian woman. He didn't look angry, exactly, but grim. Dangerous, maybe.

"You're overstepping yourself, baby sister," he said. "Do you really think it's a good idea to come on my property and attack one of my people?"

She just stared at him, her face impassive. Felix realized his mouth was gaping open. He closed it and tried to figure out when, exactly, his life had become so damn weird.

Poppy strode out onto the terrace, her heels clacking on the thin slate tiles. She looked from Young and Felix to Sparky, then down at the broken chunks of flesh on the ground.

She walked to Sparky's side, then placed her hand on his arm and gave it a gentle squeeze. He glanced at her, and some wordless communication seemed to pass between them. He shook his head, as if shrugging off a bad thought.

"She's a temp," he said to the one-armed woman. "And she shouldn't have tried to touch you. So I'm going to let this pass."

She still didn't say anything. Sparky adjusted his suit jacket, tugged his cuffs into place. "Take off," he said to her. "Keep in mind, you wouldn't get out of this building if I didn't want you to leave."

Another near-smile. "I have no doubt about that, Sparky. Shall we, Felix?"

Felix looked at Sparky, uncertain. Sparky smiled at him, relaxed and friendly once more. "Nice talking with you, Felix. We'll finish this later."

Poppy stepped forward. "I'll walk you out," she said to the woman.

With a wan smile at Sparky, Felix followed Poppy through the terrace door and over to the elevator. The one-armed woman kept very close to him; Felix couldn't decide whether her presence was reassuring or disconcerting.

The elevator doors slid open. Poppy smiled at him. "After you," she said.

The lights were out in the elevator again. Felix stood in darkness, wedged between Poppy and the other woman, feeling jumpy and vaguely queasy.

Poppy didn't speak until they were in the lobby. For the first time, she seemed angry. "For crying out loud, that wasn't smart. Don't you know better than to pick a fight with Sparky?"

"I don't like being grabbed," the woman said, her tone flat and cold.

"She couldn't have done anything to you, and you know it." Poppy shook her head furiously, her bobbed copper hair swirling around her face. "If you and Sparky start butting heads, whose side do you think I'm going to take?"

"This isn't really about you, Poppy," the woman said.

Poppy just snorted at that. After a moment, the woman shrugged. "Okay, sorry. I didn't mean to put you in an awkward position."

"There's no need for us to work at cross purposes, Young," Poppy said.

Young. "You're Young Park?" Felix asked the woman.

Poppy frowned. "You don't know her?"

"She's been following me for a couple of days, but I don't know why," Felix said.

"Nice going, Young," Poppy said. "Was there some reason for that, or did you just decide poor Felix didn't have enough weirdness in his life right now?"

"His roommate asked me to keep him out of trouble," Young said.

"Yeah? Job well done. Pat yourself on the back." Poppy shook her head, then turned to Felix. She smiled at him, reassuring and charming once more. "Sorry about all this, Felix. That got a little messier upstairs than I would have liked, but none of it needs to bother you. It was nice meeting you."

"You, too," Felix said.

"Be careful, Young," Poppy said, a warning note in her voice. She stepped back onto the dark elevator.

Once outside the building, in the hot afternoon air, Felix felt a delayed response to the charged atmosphere on the terrace. His legs shook, and he wanted to sit down on the stairs and rest his head between his knees.

Young was silent. When he started heading down the sidewalk in the direction of his car, she grabbed his arm and yanked him back. "This way," she said.

"I'm parked over there," he said.

Young shook her head. "I don't ride in cars," she said. "Anyway, it's too hard finding parking downtown. We're taking the subway."

"I'm not going downtown," Felix said. "I need to get back to work. I'm on my lunch break. I work on a TV show, and I've got a live broadcast this afternoon. I'll get fired if I miss it."

She didn't seem to be paying attention. Still pulling on his arm, she started walking in the other direction. "I'm going to take you to see Michael."

"You know where he is?" he asked. Something dawned on him. "Jamie. You and Jamie have been hiding Michael, haven't you?"

She didn't answer. He fell into stride with her. "I've been worried sick about Michael. I've been *hurt*, physically beaten and burned by people looking for him, and no one thought to tell me?"

"That's pretty much it." She threw him a cold glance. "If your feelings are hurt, take it up with Jamie. I don't actually care."

At the Metro station on Western, they climbed into a nearly empty train car, clean and air-conditioned. Felix gingerly took a seat beside Young. "How long have you been dating Jamie?" he asked.

She didn't answer. He tried again. "Are you the one he's opening the restaurant for?"

She looked at him, brow furrowed. "What?"

"His restaurant. He's opening a Korean restaurant on La Brea. 'Young Park' is a Korean name, right? He said he was doing it to impress a girl." Young looked blank at this. "Maybe I shouldn't have mentioned it."

Young was quiet for a while. "Huh," she said at last.

Felix glanced around, making sure no one could overhear their conversation. "Back there on the terrace. That woman's face shattered."

"Yep."

"Did you know that would happen if you hit her?" Felix asked.

"It seemed entirely possible," Young said. Her tone was dry. "What was she?"

"I don't know. I don't know what foul corner Sparky finds his employees in. Don't want to know."

"You and Poppy seemed to know each other," Felix said.

"Poppy doesn't count," Young said. "She's not really an employee. She's more like his . . ." She paused, considering.

"Girlfriend?"

"I can't even begin to tell you all the things wrong with that suggestion," Young said. "I guess *consigliere* is the term I want, though even that doesn't seem quite right. But Poppy and I go way back. Alhambra. Lived on the same block, went to the same school. Dated the same boys." The corner of Young's mouth quirked up, as though some memory had occurred to her.

Stations flew by. A few people got on, a few people got off. Felix glanced around. "Are we going to Pasadena?" he asked.

"Downtown, like I said. Why Pasadena?"

"Isn't that what Sparky said? 'Go back to Pasadena, princess'."

"Ah. Right. That was Sparky being a dick. About twenty years ago I was a Rose Princess. You know, the Rose Parade? Pasadena?"

A Rose Princess. Felix looked at her wounded eye, the pinned sleeve hiding the missing arm. "Can I ask . . . ?"

"Accident." It was abrupt. "Someone changed lanes on the 405 without looking."

"That's why you don't get into cars?"

"Can you blame me?" Young asked. "What did Sparky want with you?"

"He's searching for the people who are after Michael. He said he wants them to get out of town."

Young looked at him. Beneath the ice, there seemed to be something resembling concern in her expression. "He didn't hurt you, did he?"

The question startled Felix. "Sparky? No, there wasn't anything like that. He was nice enough. He's just strange. He showed me . . ." He stopped.

"What did he show you?" Young asked.

A flicker of a distant memory drifted through his brain on a fuzzy cloud. Something about a windowless room, and cages, and birds. "I don't remember," he said.

Young frowned, but didn't say anything.

CHAPTER EIGHTEEN

THEY GOT OFF the train at the Civic Center, next to City Hall and all the pretty government buildings. Young started walking south, with Felix at her side, until they crossed into the neighborhood he'd visited just yesterday, near the *Anathema* set.

"This is Skid Row, right?" he asked. He tried to keep his tone casual.

Young hadn't said anything since they left the subway. She gave him a curt nod.

"You live here?" he asked.

"Yeah," she said. It was almost a growl.

"You've been hiding my brother on Skid Row?"

She didn't say anything, and at first Felix thought he'd offended her. At long last, she smiled without looking at him. "Mr. Judgmental," she said.

"Sorry." He trailed her down empty sidewalks. That was the weird part about Skid Row, how vacant it was. Just a lot of boarded and shuttered buildings, no cars on the street. "Is it always this quiet?"

"LAPD doesn't like people loitering on the sidewalk. They come through a few times a day and shoo everyone off." She frowned and looked around. "Problem is, most of the people around here don't have anywhere else to go. So they trickle back as soon as the coast is clear."

"Do you live on the street?" he asked.

"Not now. Here I am." She jerked her head at a nondescript four-story stucco building, the front windows blocked out by yellowed newspapers. An iron gate protected the stoop. The gate was unlocked; Young pushed it open and climbed up the cracked concrete steps.

Felix followed her into a dingy yellow lobby. A row of metal mailboxes were hammered crudely into the wall, their doors all missing. A graying woman in a sleeveless checkered shift sat at a counter behind a thick, scratched acrylic window. Next to the window, a barred security door separated the lobby from the rest of the building. The woman looked at Felix and Young, her expression impassive, then pressed a button on the counter. A buzzer sounded, and Young pushed open the now-unlocked door.

He followed her in silence up a creaky flight of stairs to the second floor. The nylon carpet in the hallway was fraying along the edges, and the walls were in need of a fresh coat of paint.

She unlocked a battered wooden door at the far end of the hall and ushered Felix inside. He took in the peeling paint, the water damage on the ceiling, the lack of furniture, the stacks of battered paperback books and newspapers lining the walls. There was a small open kitchenette with a sink and a yellow refrigerator attached to the living room.

Jamie stood at the vinyl countertop in the kitchenette, stirring something in a sauce pot on a hot plate plugged into the wall. He twisted his head and looked at Felix in surprise.

He wasn't alone. Michael sat on the counter next to the hot plate, kicking his heels against the cupboards. Sharp relief blended with an equally sharp flare of anger as Felix looked at him.

Michael stopped swinging his legs. He opened his mouth. After a moment of silence, he managed to say something. "Oh."

Jamie glanced at Young. "I thought we weren't going to tell him."

"He went to see Sparky Mother. I had to intervene." She closed and locked the door, then applied the chain lock.

"Holy crap." Jamie stared at Felix, then back at Young. "What's Sparky's involvement in this?"

"Who's Sparky Mother?" Michael asked. He hopped down off the counter.

Nobody answered him. Jamie raised the wooden spoon out of the sauce pot and set it on the counter. Something bright yellow and sticky clung to the spoon. Macaroni and cheese. The kind that came in a box, the kind with the fluorescent powdered cheese. The really good kind.

"Why didn't anyone let me know about this?" Felix asked.

"It was my idea to bring Mike here, after he told me what was going on," Jamie said. "Young's been keeping him safe."

"Okay, fine, but he's my brother. Why wouldn't you tell me?"

"It's a very good thing I didn't." Jamie sounded patient, but cold. "You would have told Claire and Nicky where he was when they tortured you, and then they would've killed you."

"They tortured you?" Michael looked at Felix, his eyes wide. "You told me they didn't hurt you."

"And you told me you were in Chicago." It came out bitchy and petulant, and Felix was aware of a growing urge to pitch a full-scale hissyfit. The way Michael and Jamie had quietly formed an alliance without him, the way he was so obviously inessential to their plans, it all rankled him to his core.

"Why did you go see Sparky Mother?" Jamie asked.

"Because his assistant called and told me to." Felix felt exhausted and crabby. Jamie's macaroni smelled like it was burning. Felix's stomach growled.

"Who's Sparky Mother?" Michael asked again.

Once again, nobody answered. Young prowled around her apartment and pulled the shade lower across the single window.

Jamie looked down at the pot. He cursed and unplugged the hot plate from the wall. "Lunch is ready, or slightly past ready. Why don't we compare notes over food?"

Young glanced into the pot. "I know I didn't have any milk."

"I used those individual cartons of non-dairy creamer in your fridge. I meant to bring groceries. I tried ordering pizza, but no one would deliver to this block." Jamie scooped the macaroni into whatever serving vessels he could find. Before Felix could tell him he didn't want any, he was presented with a portion in a plastic coffee mug emblazoned with the words "Hemodonor Plasma Center" on the side.

"You don't need to buy me food," Young said. It was curt.

"I know. I was thinking mostly of Mike. He says he's been eating a lot of instant soup lately." Jamie handed her a bowl of macaroni. She accepted it wordlessly. Felix observed them standing beside each other at the hot plate, shoulder to shoulder without quite touching. As a couple, they were a decent match, visually: Young was probably close to Jamie's age, and her bleached hair and raggedy trench coat weren't too dissimilar from Jamie's own personal style. There was a distance to Young, though, a closed-off remoteness that made Felix doubt Jamie's relationship with her, whatever it really was, would last for long.

Young leaned against the far wall by the window. She flicked the shade aside and glanced out, as though making sure no one was spying on the building. Jamie sat cross-legged on the carpet. Michael sat down beside him.

Still feeling like an outsider to their private club, Felix sat by the door. He shifted aside a stack of pornographic newspapers, of the variety distributed for free throughout the city, the ones that consisted mostly of ads for escort services. It was an awfully big stack. He looked at Young.

"My day job," she said in answer to his unasked question. She gestured at the papers. "I write the movie reviews."

"That could be fun," Felix said. He smiled at her. There was no answering smile. He took a bite of his macaroni to disguise his sudden embarrassment Heavenly, even though it was noticeably scorched. Salty, fatty, chemical-laden goodness rolled across his tongue and exploded in his mouth.

"So here's what we know," Jamie said. "We know there's two of them, Claire and Nicky, and we know they're after Mike, that they've followed him first from Omaha when he was a kid and more recently from Chicago. We know they're not human, but we don't know what they are."

"Sparky said they were fire demons," Felix said.

"Did he? Okay, well, he'd probably know."

"You said they come out through your chest, right?" Felix asked Michael.

"Yeah." Michael's hand went to the front of his shirt, over the weird circular patch of skin on his chest. "That's how they escape from wherever they are when they're not here."

"You stopped setting fires . . . The fires stopped eight years ago," Felix said. "They stopped after dad left. Dr. Boyd said you were finally dealing with your issues."

"It didn't have anything to do with dad, or my issues, whatever that even means. It all was because we moved into that apartment in Elkhorn. Nicky and Claire didn't know where I lived. They couldn't find me anymore."

"Okay, but that apartment was maybe twenty miles from our old house. If they couldn't find you there, how'd they track you all the way to Chicago?" Felix asked.

"Because I did something stupid," Michael said. His voice was harsh. "I got homesick this summer. My job sucked, and it was too muggy and gross in the city, and I was miserable. So I went to visit mom."

"I know. She wrote to me and mentioned that." She'd suggested that Felix visit, too, but he'd been too busy with *The Big Boom*.

"And while I was there, I went out to our old house. Just to see it. From what Claire told me later, I got back on their radar then." Michael laughed, hollow and strained. "She said I give off some kind of energy. If they concentrate on it, they can track me down wherever I am. So they followed me from Omaha to Chicago and burst out through my chest. They set my sofa on fire. I've got a couple of roommates who probably never want to see me again."

"And so Nicky and Claire figured you'd head to Los Angeles next," Jamie said.

"Right." Michael looked glum. "I'm never going to be free of them now, am I? I can't hide from them."

Felix cleared his throat. "Claire's gone," he said. "I don't know if Jamie told you. She burned up or melted or something.

152

So I guess we don't have to worry about her. Just Nicky." He supposed that was a good thing, but the thought of Claire's destruction, her wail of agony and the flames that consumed her while he stood and watched, made him feel cold and sick.

"She'll come back, that's what I've been saying. They don't seem to last very long in this world—just a matter of days, or maybe weeks—but they can use me to return. They can locate me whether they're in this world or their world, doesn't matter. Claire's probably locking for me right now." Michael shivered and drew his knees up to his chest.

Silence hung in the room. Young shifted against the wall. "Sparky knows I'm involved in this. Michael isn't safe here anymore."

"Yeah. Felix, what did Sparky want with you anyway?" Jamie asked.

"He wants Claire and Nicky out of the city. He said either Michael could get out of town and let them follow him, or . . ." He trailed off.

"Or he'd kill Mike, is that it?" Jamie said.

"I think so. He didn't say that in so many words, but that's the impression I got."

"Sparky didn't hurt you, did he?" Jamie asked.

Young had asked the same thing. Felix thought back to the strange encounter. There'd been danger there, but none of it had been directed at him. In fact, he had the crazy impression that Sparky liked him. And Poppy had been charming. "No. He seemed okay. Who is he?"

"Young? You want to take this one?" Jamie asked.

Young shifted. She looked uncomfortable for the first time, as though this was a subject she'd rather avoid. "There's a group in Los Angeles that exerts a lot of control over various aspects of the city. Think of it like a top-secret City Council, except instead of geographical districts, it's divided up by people, or by industries. Sparky Mother is in charge of everyone who works in the entertainment industry." She shrugged. "Since this is L.A., that means he has the most power."

"That's probably why he approached Felix," Jamie said. "You work in television, so you're one of his constituents."

"You're one of them, aren't you?" Felix asked Young. "Sparky said something like that, about how I don't fall under you. And he called you 'baby sister'."

Young's visible discomfort increased. "Yeah. I'm new though. Poppy nominated me for the position. I represent the . . . well, I'd say 'homeless', except a lot of us have places to live. I guess my constituents, if we're calling them that, would be the disenfranchised people of the city. The leftovers." She smiled, dark and wry. "It's an awfully big group. Larger than the entertainment industry, but we wield far less influence."

"What do you have to do?" Felix asked.

"Not sure yet. I'm supposed to look out for everyone's best interests, but nobody's explained how I should go about doing that. Poppy assures me it'll become obvious as I go along."

Felix cleared his throat. "So I think it's pretty clear that Sparky is something supernatural, right?"

"I don't know what he is. Poppy has implied that asking questions about Sparky is not encouraged."

"Are you?" Felix asked. "Supernatural?"

She shook her head. "I can't do anything. I don't know why I have this position. I don't know what I'm supposed to do." She sounded frustrated.

"There's what you told me," Jamie said quietly.

She looked at him, and her expression softened a little. "Yeah. But I don't know if that has anything to do with it."

She turned to Felix. "Jamie's talking about my accident. I was dead at the scene, paramedics brought me back. But sometimes it feels like part of me got left behind."

"What does that mean?" Felix asked. Across the room, Michael was motionless. It was hard to tell how much of this he'd already heard, or how much he understood or believed. Then again, Michael had been living with irrefutable knowledge of strange, scary forces in the world from a very young age.

And Felix had never listened to him.

Young's expression grew distant. "Just sometimes when I'm tired or sick or really focused on some project, it seems like I'm in a different place. I'm not sure where it is, but I'm whole there, I have my arm back and my face isn't messed up. If I have any power, it's there, if I can figure out how to get there."

"Do you think that place might be where they live?" Michael asked. "Claire and Nicky. Because if so, I think I'm some kind of gateway to it."

"Could be. I don't really know." She shook her head. "I don't like talking about it."

"Who are the others?" Felix asked. "The other members of this council, I mean."

"I don't know. It's not like we have meetings. I know there's a guy who controls the beach culture—surfers and lifeguards and stuff like that. Poppy said they had problems with him a couple years back. He got into some big fight with Sparky, so he's been laying low."

A shadowy organization secretly controlling Los Angeles . . . "This is *Anathema*," Felix said.

Everyone turned to him, confused. "What?" Jamie asked.

155

Felix felt his face turn red. "*Anathema*. It's the plot of a TV show." He shook his head. "Never mind. It doesn't matter."

He glanced down at his watch as a sudden thought struck him. It was almost three. "Crap. I need to get back to work. I'm going to miss my broadcast."

"Skip it," Jamie said. "This is more important."

"I'll get fired," Felix said. "I'll come straight back here after the show. Michael's probably safe here for another couple of hours, right?"

"Not if Sparky knows he's with me," Young said. "We have to move him."

"Then he can come with me," Felix said. "He can hang out at my desk while I do the broadcast. We'll figure out what to do after that."

"Okay, that works," Jamie said. "Let's get you packed up and out of here, Mike."

"Where am I going to go?" Michael asked. "I'm not safe anywhere."

"I know. We'll work something out. Right now, let's focus on keeping you away from Sparky," Jamie said.

Michael exhaled, then nodded and got to his feet. "Okay," he said. "Felix, you want to help me pack?"

The apartment's tiny, windowless bedroom, like the rest of the apartment, was unfurnished. A blanket was folded up in the corner. Felix looked around. "Rustic," he said.

"You're telling me. I've been using my backpack as a pillow."

"Where does Young sleep?" Felix asked.

"Young doesn't sleep." Michael almost smiled. "Young prowls. She'd check in with me during the day, and Jamie's been here off and on, but she doesn't spend a lot of time here. I don't know where she goes."

"She was following me part of the time," Felix said. "What have you been doing for the past few days?"

"Eating ramen and reading porn, mostly. I'm very happy this phase of my adventure is drawing to a close." He looked at Felix. "I'm sorry they hurt you because of me."

"It's not your fault," Felix said. "I'm sorry I never believed you about the fires."

"Yeah, well, fire demons burrowing out of my chest is maybe not the most obvious explanation." Michael shrugged. "It's okay. It sucked at the time that you didn't have faith in me, but I get it. It was a whole lot easier to believe I was a pyro. I think I almost started believing it myself."

Felix couldn't answer that. He sat and watched Michael stuff his clothes into his backpack.

CHAPTER NINETEEN

JAMIE DROPPED FELIX and Michael off at Felix's car, which was still parked near Sparky's office. He'd offered to drive them straight to Atomic, but Felix, who was still feeling prickly and resentful at the way Jamie and Michael had left him out of their plans, turned him down.

The more he mulled it over, though, the more he realized he was being an ass. Michael had been in grave danger—still was, in fact—and this really wasn't about Felix at all. Which was maybe the source of his pique.

Jamie let them out at the curb. "Go straight home after the broadcast," he told them. "If anything weird happens, call me right away, okay?"

"Sure," Felix said.

"Hang in there, Mike. We'll figure out some way to work this out." Jamie waited until Felix and Michael were safely inside Felix's car before driving off.

Michael shot Felix a sidelong glance. "You're awfully quiet. You mad at me?"

"Not really. Not for anything that's your fault, at least." Felix glanced up at Sparky's building, still run-down and outwardly deserted, and felt a chill.

His car was junky and comforting. He settled into the driver's seat. "Seatbelts," he said.

The clock on his dashboard read 3:20. He had time to make it to the studio, even if they were caught in traffic. He'd get in trouble for his lengthy absence—a quick glance at his phone showed he'd already missed three calls from Curt—but he wouldn't miss the broadcast. It'd be okay.

"I didn't want any of this to happen," Michael said. He held his bulky backpack in his lap, his hands twisting the straps in agitation. "I'm really scared."

"I know. But Jamie's right. We're going to figure something out, okay?"

"Did that guy—Stubby Mother—tell you anything about why this is happening to me?"

"Sparky. Sparky Mother." He pulled out of his parking space. "Yeah, sort of. He thought you might have some demon blood in you."

"What?"

"It's his theory, at least. He might be full of crap." Felix glanced at his brother. "He suggested you and I might have different fathers."

Michael opened his mouth to reply, then his eyes widened. "Felix!"

Felix looked up to see a white SUV bearing down on them, heading the wrong direction down the one-way street at a high speed. There wasn't enough room to swerve out of the way, so he jerked the wheel hard to the right, driving up onto the sidewalk and clipping a street sign in the process before coming to a stop.

His heart pounded in staccato bursts from the adrenaline surge. He clutched the steering wheel so tightly he didn't know if he'd ever be able to uncurl his fingers again. "Michael? You okay?"

"I'm fine. What the hell was that driver doing?"

The SUV stopped in the middle of the street. The driver emerged. A young man with sandy hair, and while he didn't look exactly like Nicky, the look of fury on his face left no doubt as to his identification.

"It's Nicky," Felix said, his voice little more than a gasp. "Lock your—"

The passenger door flew open. Nicky reached in, unbuckled Michael's seatbelt, and dragged him out by the hair. He threw him to the sidewalk. Before Michael could react, Nicky crouched down and smashed his head against the pavement.

Felix unfastened his own seatbelt and climbed out through the passenger side. He launched himself at Nicky's back. His car keys were clenched in his fist, so he tried to use them as a weapon, tried to stab at his neck, his back. "Leave him alone!"

Nicky shrugged him off. When Michael tried to lift his head up, Nicky smashed it against the sidewalk once more. Michael lay still.

Nicky faced Felix. His face was dark red, his eyes barely slits, his mouth an angry twist. He looked at him and said one word: "*You.*"

A blast of lethal malice was condensed into one syllable, a deadly missile aimed at Felix. Nicky sprang at him, and Felix bolted.

He sprinted toward Wilshire, legs moving so fast it was a miracle he didn't pitch forward and land on his face. Nicky was right behind him, and that was terrible for many reasons, but at least he was leading Nicky away from Michael.

At Wilshire, there'd be cars and people, and maybe he could find help there. His thoughts immediately went to Sparky. Jamie and Young had warned him about Sparky, but he was clearly powerful, and if Felix could make it inside his office building . . .

The fence surrounding the building was chained shut and padlocked, but it looked like it could be scaled easily enough. Before Felix could reach it, Nicky tackled him from the side and threw him onto his back on the sidewalk.

For a moment Felix couldn't breathe, the wind knocked from his lungs. It felt like falling off the monkey bars on the grade school playground.

"You stupid little fuckwit," Nicky said, his voice scarcely more than a hiss. "You destroyed her, didn't you? It was you, I know it was you."

"I didn't mean to." There, he could speak. That must mean he was breathing again. "She caught on fire, and then she melted, but it was an accident, I swear. I tried to help her." Knowing as he spoke that it was useless, that Nicky wouldn't care if it was an accident or not. That Nicky was going to kill him anyway.

Nicky knelt over him, knees straddling his sides. His face was grotesque, distorted with rage. "You destroyed her," he said. "What do you think I'm going to do to you for that? I'm going to bash in your face, break all those nice teeth."

Felix's car keys were still clenched in his hand. He gripped them between his fingers and lashed out at Nicky's face.

The tips of his keys slashed his jaw. A jagged red line appeared in the skin, and the flesh across his chin started to pull apart in sticky threads like melting taffy. From under his skin, something glowed bright orange.

Nicky grunted. He brought his hands to his chin and pressed the edges of the cut back together. Little bits of flame

161

appeared between his fingers, which he smothered with his hands as quickly as they appeared. He sealed the cut and smoothed it out with his fingers. "Nice try," he said. He rose to his feet and drew his leg back.

Felix's jaw exploded in a supernova of pain. Nicky's first kick was followed by another kick to his ribs. Another explosion of agony. And another.

He didn't feel the fourth kick so much. He wasn't feeling much of anything anymore. That was worrisome, but okay. It was nice, in fact. He was floating somewhere far away, somewhere without pain, where everything was dark and quiet.

He stayed in the dark place as long as he could, floating in the silent void, returning only when something cold landed on his chest and jolted him back to consciousness. He opened his eyes. The pain returned with the rest of his senses.

Someone stood over him, someone who wasn't Nicky. Felix's eyes slowly adjusted on Sparky. He crouched down beside Felix. "How you doing, Omaha?"

"Michael," Felix said, or tried to say. Couldn't open his jaw, couldn't move his mouth without a wave of nausea-inducing pain. He tried to focus on the object Sparky had dropped on him. A cold square of blue plastic.

"Don't speak," Sparky said. "Use that." He gestured at the object.

Felix looked up at him, not able to ask him what he meant. Sparky shook his head in what looked like affectionate exasperation and picked up the blue square. Through the haze of pain that was clouding his thoughts, Felix finally managed to identify it. A chemical ice pack.

"Here," Sparky said. He slipped an arm under Felix's back and raised him up to a sitting position. Felix wanted to tell him to

162

be careful, that all kinds of things inside of him had been smashed and he really shouldn't be moved at all, but words were far beyond him, especially with his broken jaw.

The gate to the chain-link fence was now unlocked and stood open. Sparky, still in his expensive suit, sat down on the trash-strewn sidewalk. He leaned back against the fence and propped Felix against his shoulder, holding him upright with his arm around his waist. He placed the ice pack against Felix's jaw. Felix flinched. There was a brief cold sensation, and then the blinding pain vanished.

"Better?" Sparky asked. Felix was too startled and confused to even nod. Sparky dropped the ice pack into his lap. "Use that on your ribs."

He fumbled to pick up the pack with clumsy fingers. He slipped it under his shirt and pressed it against his busted ribs.

He could feel things moving on his skin and under his skin, ribs knitting back together, scrapes and bruises healing, the damage undoing itself. He shifted the pack and moved it across his abdomen until all the pain was gone.

"Michael," he said, now that he could speak. "Where's Michael, is he okay?"

Sparky shook his head. "Gone. He got him. He took off in your car when he saw me, took your brother along for the ride."

Felix looked around. His head swam when he moved. His car keys were missing. "He hurt Michael really badly. He smashed his head into the sidewalk," he said. "He might've killed him."

"Nope. Your brother's tougher than that. If he can survive a couple of fire demons bursting out of his chest every now and again, he can take a few blows. Better than you can, that's for sure."

"It was more than a few blows," Felix said. "He kicked the crap out of me."

"That he did." Felix wasn't looking at him, but it sounded like Sparky was smiling. "Your brother's okay. He's too valuable to them to kill, and in any case, it sounds like he's more or less immune to whatever they can do to him. If he's got some demon blood in him, maybe he can heal up quickly. Hey, are you feeling like you can stand?"

"I think so, yeah. Thank you for fixing me," Felix said. With Sparky's help, he got to his feet. His legs wobbled, and his head felt much heavier than his body, but all the pain was gone. He looked down at the ice pack in his hand. "Did this do it, or was it you?"

Sparky smiled. He reached out with two fingers and touched Felix's jaw. There was a faint tingle at the touch, an electric charge that didn't burn. The beautiful blue eyes glittered. "What do you think?"

"Will you help me get Michael back?" Felix asked.

Sparky regarded Felix in silence for a moment, then shook his head. "It's not what I do," he said. "If you need to ace an audition, or impress a director, something along those lines, I can come in very, very handy. Maybe someday when you're less distracted, you and I will work something out. But right now, for this, you're on your own."

"You're more powerful than they are, aren't you?"

"By a factor of like eight billion, yeah. But again, smacking down the junior varsity players isn't really what I do. Not to sound too terribly grand, but paying too much attention to them is beneath me."

"You want them to leave town. That's what you told me earlier," Felix said. "You want to get back at them for killing Chad and Timothy. They both worked in entertainment, you're responsible for them, right? It's in your best interests to help me."

"You don't understand what you're asking," Sparky said. He spoke quietly, his expression unreadable. "And everybody, always, understands what they're getting into with me."

"Then what can I do?" Felix asked. There was a dangerous lump forming in his throat.

Sparky shrugged. "He kidnapped your brother and stole your car. What you should probably do is call the police."

"The police?" Felix asked. "What are the police going to do about a fire demon?"

"Don't underestimate the LAPD. This is Los Angeles. There's very little they haven't seen, and they can be mighty useful in situations like this." He grinned. "Just a suggestion, though, maybe leave out the word 'demon' when you talk to them, if you want them to take you seriously. And here."

He withdrew a pale blue business card from his inner jacket pocket and handed it to Felix. Sparky Mother, it said, with a phone number. It had a logo of a little cartoon tiger carrying a firecracker.

It was far and away the dumbest business card Felix had ever seen.

Sparky nodded at the card. "After all this is over, after you've gotten yourself well and truly shitcanned from Atomic, give me a call. We can talk over the next stage of your career."

"After I get shitcanned?" His muscles felt stiff, as though they were clinging to the memory of a pain that was no longer there.

"You're supposed to be on the air in twenty minutes. Unless you can teleport, you're going to miss a live broadcast. Somehow

165

I think that's going to be the nail in your coffin at the network." Sparky touched two fingers to his forehead in a salute. "See you around, Felix."

With that, he walked up the broken and dirty front stairs of his office building.

CHAPTER TWENTY

THE FIRST CALL Felix made was to Jamie, briefing him on the situation and agreeing to meet him and Young back at the duplex. The second call was to the police.

The policeman who arrived, Officer Downs, was young and kind. He was reed-slender, with dark skin and sad eyes and a razor-thin mustache. He let Felix sit in his air-conditioned patrol car and listened to Felix's judiciously-edited story about Nicky's attack and Michael's kidnapping. He entered his notes directly into his dashboard computer.

"Why were you and your brother here?" Downs asked. His tone seemed no more than curious.

Felix paused. "I had an appointment in this building," he said.

Downs looked at the unprepossessing structure, at the chain-link fence out front and the soaped-over windows. "Here?"

"Yeah." Felix swallowed. "I know it looks like it's abandoned, but there are offices on the higher levels. Legitimate businesses," he added, because Downs was starting to look a little suspicious about whatever business would take place in this kind of building.

"Who were you seeing?"

"His name's Sparky Mother," Felix said. "He's an important shareholder in Atomic, the network I've been working for. They've been considering whether to offer me a permanent position, and Sparky wanted to meet me."

"Can you spell that name?" Downs asked. "Is that Mother, or . . . ?"

"Mother. Like, mother. Mom. I don't know if Sparky is his real name, but that's what he goes by."

Downs nodded. "Hang on a minute," he said. He continued typing into the dashboard computer. From the passenger seat, Felix couldn't read what he was writing. After a long pause, he looked up at Felix. "Can you come down to the station with me? It's not far."

"Yeah." He was missing his broadcast, his career at Atomic was over, and it didn't matter at all.

They drove to the station on south Vermont. The glass building was new and glossy and looked more like a public library or community center than Felix's idea of what an urban police station should look like. Downs took him behind the front counter into a maze of gray cubicles. He pointed to a chair. "Take a seat and hang out for a minute. I'm going to find someone to talk to you. You need coffee?"

"No, thanks." Felix sat. Downs's desk was small and cluttered with leaning stacks of thick file folders. Felix waited for far too long and tried to keep calm. Downs said he'd put an APB on Felix's car. Maybe they'd find it, and maybe the police would be able to stop Nicky before Michael got hurt. Or maybe Jamie and Young would figure out how to track down Nicky. None of it seemed likely, but it wasn't like he had any idea what to do, so it didn't really matter that he was stuck here, wasting time.

At an adjacent cubicle, a young woman sobbed openly, her head in her hands. Without lifting her head, she said something in a torrent of Spanish to the officer occupying the desk. Felix felt like doing the same, breaking down and crying until all of the fear and worry and misery was drained out of him.

"You Felix?" He looked up.

A young woman in a navy pantsuit stood beside him. She had long brown hair winched off her face in a tight low ponytail, huge brown eyes, and a tiny mouth drawn into a firm line. "I'm Detective Guerrero. Can you follow me?"

She led him into a small conference room and gestured for him to take a seat. She wasn't carrying a file or any kind of paperwork that he could see, and for a glum moment Felix thought he might be expected to tell his story all over again.

She sat across from him and stared at him, her lovely face grim. She exhaled. "Okay, so look: I'm not assigned to your brother's case, and I know you got like a million things you're worried about right now, so I'm real sorry that my timing is bad. I can promise you, other detectives are out there right now looking around the city for Mike, okay?"

"I guess," Felix said. "If you're not assigned to the case, why am I here?"

She chewed on her bottom lip. "There's this other deal I'm working on, this case I've been following for a couple of years now. And the guy in the case, you mentioned his name when Downs interviewed you."

Oh. "Sparky Mother?"

"Got it in one." She smiled. "Any time that name comes up in a file, I get notified. So look, nobody says you have to talk to me right now, but you could really help me out."

"I doubt it," Felix said. "I just met Sparky today. I don't know anything about him."

"But you knew right away I was talking about him, right? You know he's the kind of guy the cops might be looking into." She shrugged. "Look, believe me, I'm not looking to get you into any trouble, okay? But if you're cool with it, I think there's someone you should meet."

Felix shook his head. "I'd rather not."

"Please." The sudden desperation in her tone surprised him. "Please. It's not just for my case. This could help you. Might even save your life."

"I don't know what you're talking about," Felix said.

"Don't you?" Guerrero slid back in her chair. "If you genuinely don't know what you're getting into with Sparky, then you should find out. The dude's bad news, and I know someone who can tell you why."

She got to her feet. "Come on. I'll drive you. When we're done, I'll drop you off wherever you want to be, and then you'll never have to think about this again."

Not entirely sure he had any choice in the matter, Felix followed her out to the parking lot. Dark clouds had moved in, and there was a new coolness to the air. Guerrero glanced up. "Damn, I think we're going to get rain, huh? Didn't see that in the forecast."

Felix didn't answer. Sparky had said it was going to start raining soon.

They drove in her unmarked sedan up to Hollywood, close to the Atomic building. To Felix's surprise, Guerrero turned into the gated driveway of a small production studio. She flashed her badge at the guard at the booth, and he raised the parking arm to let them drive onto the lot.

Felix looked around. He'd been here before, on a cattle call for a yogurt commercial. At the center of the lot were the sound stages, a cluster of gigantic white-painted buildings the size of airplane hangars. Billboards for current television shows were mounted from the tops of the buildings. Apparently *Anathema* was produced here, because there was Ridpath Washburn as Carlos Mater, dressed in an exquisite three-piece suit, looming over the lot. His hands were folded on top of a massive mahogany desk, and he was smiling with what Felix could only describe as malevolent charm

They parked in a parking structure. Guerrero strode across the lot in her sensible loafers, moving like she'd been here many times before. "Who are we here to see?" Felix asked.

She looked a little abashed. "My husband," she said. "He's got a vested interest in Sparky Mother. He's a real good person for you to talk to."

Across from the stages was a row of two-story bungalows, tidy white cottages housing the offices of production executives. Guerrero led him up to a closed door on the second level. The bronze plate beside the doorbell read *Anathema*. She stabbed a finger at the bell, then opened the door without waiting for a response.

Beyond the door was a cheerful reception area, wood floors and yellow walls and miniature orange trees in ceramic planters. A bright-eyed young man in a pale yellow shirt sat behind the reception desk. "Hi, Diana," he said. He gave a cheerful wave that seemed to include Felix as well. "He's not on the phone, so you can go on through."

"Thank you, Tad." Guerrero ushered Felix through the door behind Tad's desk.

Felix found himself in a small, cluttered office. A large *Anathema* poster, identical to the billboard that graced the outside of the stage, hung on the wall between two windows that looked out over the lot. Felix saw a row of palm trees rising up from behind several parked production trailers. The Hollywood dream was contained in this office.

Behind a desk sat a young Indian man. He was maybe in his early thirties, dark-skinned and handsome in jeans and a t-shirt. He rose to his feet at the sight of Guerrero and Felix.

"Felix, this is my husband, Vish Kuyavar. Vish, this is Felix."

"From *The Big Boom*. Sure." Vish reached over the desk to shake hands. His grip was strong. When he smiled, it seemed warm and genuine. "Felix, Diana told me about your brother. I'm very sorry. I hope he's found safely."

"Thank you," Felix said. "Me, too."

"I'll try to keep this quick. Have a seat," Vish said. He gestured to the leather chairs in front of his cluttered desk. Felix sat down. Guerrero shut the door, then slid her chair in front of it and sat, barricading the door from intruders. The motion seemed reflexive, like it was something she did all the time.

Felix glanced up at the poster. "So you work on *Anathema*?"

Vish smiled. "I created it," he said. "I'm the showrunner."

"It's a really good program. I was downtown visiting the set yesterday for my show. I met Ridpath and Charlotte," Felix said.

"I'm sorry I missed you," Vish said.

Felix pointed at the poster, at Ridpath sitting behind that huge desk. "Is Carlos Mater supposed to be Sparky Mother?"

Vish was very still. He exchanged looks with Guerrero, his expression unreadable. After a while, he turned back to Felix. "Yes," he said. "Yes, he is. Then you do know about Sparky."

"About his secret group? I know a little," Felix said. "Why are you making a show about Sparky?"

Vish smiled. It looked tense. "To get back at him," he said. "To get his attention. To get under his skin, if I can."

"Why?" Vish didn't seem like the vindictive type. And both Jamie and Young had seemed . . . well, maybe not exactly scared of Sparky, but definitely wary of him. And here Vish was, trying to provoke him.

Vish exhaled. "Maybe two years ago, I was a struggling screenwriter. Actually, that overstates the case a little, because *struggling* implies action. I was getting exactly nowhere with my writing, working as a caterer to make ends meet. And then I met Sparky." He shook his head. "I'll spare you the details. I'll just say that Sparky got me a job writing for a show, *Interstellar Boys*."

"That's where you met Ridpath?"

Vish nodded. "Long story short, it turns out Sparky was using me as a pawn in some feud he was having with one of his more charming associates. I almost got killed in the process. A lot of people did get killed, actually."

His tone was matter-of-fact. He seemed very composed. "Sparky offered to make it up to me afterward. He promised to help me get a nice career in the industry. I turned him down, repeatedly and emphatically. I went back to catering and tried to forget about him."

There was something a little hypnotic about Vish's calm narrative. "So maybe a month after that, I got offered a job from the head of production here. They were willing to let me develop any television show I wanted. Loose purse strings, full creative freedom. Hence, *Anathema*. And I'm pretty sure I know who to thank for all this." He gestured around his office.

In front of the door, Guerrero shifted in her seat. "Look up Sparky online sometime. I bet you won't find any search results for his name. Or if you find something, it's because he wants you to find it. Leaving you a breadcrumb trail. Write something about him on a website, and it'll get mysteriously deleted. That police report Downs filed about your brother, the one where you mentioned Sparky, I'll pull it tomorrow, and Sparky's name will be gone. He's *connected*."

Felix stared at her. "Sparky suggested I call the police," he said. "It didn't seem like he'd care if I mentioned him."

"Did he? That's interesting," Vish said.

"What does it mean?"

"It probably means he wanted you to talk to me," Vish said. "He knows what Diana and I are doing. He knows everything. I'm sure he's been keeping tabs on me."

"Yeah, but . . . " Felix thought for a moment about how to phrase it. "*Anathema* is a great show. Everybody's sure it's going to win a bunch of Emmys next week. It sounds like Sparky maybe felt bad about putting you in danger, so he pulled some strings to get you this job. Maybe I'm missing something, but I don't really see anything *evil* about it."

"I know. I don't see anything evil about it, either. That's the thing. It seems great, right? My life is so much better for having known Sparky," Vish said. "But maybe all this is going to come at a cost, and I don't know what it's going to be."

His tone grew sharp. For the first time, Felix realized there was anger to Vish beneath his calm, genial exterior, as well as faint traces of some unattractive bitterness. More than that, though, Vish was deeply, profoundly frightened.

"Does Sparky have anything to do with your brother's kidnapping?" Guerrero asked.

Felix shook his head. "Absolutely not. Not at all."

"How do you know about him? How did you make the *Anathema* connection?" she asked. "You said you just met him today. Did he tell you all that?"

"No, it's . . ." He thought of Young, in her shabby apartment, confused and frustrated about her baffling new role on Sparky's council. "I can't tell you."

"In addition to Sparky, I've met two of them," Vish said. "There's a creature that runs the beaches. It takes human form sometimes, but it lives under the earth near the water, and it's definitely not human. It doesn't get along with Sparky. I got caught up in the middle of a fight between them. You remember that big news story a couple years ago, about all those actors they found dead in a cave?"

"Uh-huh. Of course. It was a gang of surfers who killed them, right?"

"The surfers were working for the creature. He did it to get Sparky's attention. Sparky got mad about it, so he got his revenge. He murdered all of them. I was there when he did it."

"Really?" Felix gaped at him. "That doesn't seem right. I can't picture Sparky getting his hands dirty like that. He's not the type."

"Oh, he didn't need to use his hands." Vish's smile was cool. "He looked at the surfers, and they caught on fire. They burned to death right in front of me."

Felix couldn't answer. Vish observed him with what seemed like compassion, then continued. "And there's a lawyer who works downtown, Isabella Madre. She's another one. She's in charge of looking after all the immigrants in the city. I wouldn't say she's friendly, exactly, but I think she's a good person. If she *is* a person."

"Vish and I are trying to identify the others," Guerrero said. "All the members of Sparky's council. Do you know any of them?"

"I don't know anything." Felix got to his feet. "I really have to go. My brother—"

"I know. I'm sorry. I won't keep you," Vish said. "You have no reason to trust me, but if you ever feel like talking more about this, my door is always open."

"In the meantime, stay away from Sparky," Guerrero said. "He may seem like an okay guy, all charming and shit, but you don't want to get mixed up with him. Dude's got too much power."

And what Felix needed right now, more than anything, was power. He didn't say that, though, and just nodded at Vish and Guerrero in what he hoped looked like agreement.

CHAPTER TWENTY-ONE

THE SILENCE WAS awkward in Guerrero's car, as though they'd shared too much back in Vish's office. "Where can I drop you, Felix?" she asked.

"My workplace. Atomic, just over near Van Ness," he said. "I missed the show this afternoon because of all this. I should throw myself on their mercy."

"You had a good reason," she said. She shrugged. "I'd say I'm sure they'll understand your situation, but I know something about Hollywood types from being around Vish. It's entirely possible they'll be dickwads about it."

"How'd you and Vish meet?" he asked.

She grinned for the first time. "We seem an odd pairing, huh? Hollywood player and LAPD detective, right?" She considered. "We met through this, really. Sparky, I mean. I was a beat cop in Venice, and Vish got caught up in some pretty scary shit that we were investigating. That's what he was talking about back there, the thing with the surfers. After the investigation was closed, we figured out we had some common interests."

She pulled onto the parking ramp at Atomic and stopped just before the guard booth. "This is you."

"Thank you," Felix said. He climbed out of the passenger seat. She leaned over and spoke through the open window.

"They give you any crap about missing work, call the desk and ask for a copy of your police report. Your bosses might cut you a little slack." She nodded at him. "I hope your brother gets found safe. See you around, Felix. And stay away from Sparky, okay?"

Felix waited until she'd pulled back into the traffic on Sunset. He stared up at the building. He could see if Curt was still in his office and try to explain the situation.

Caring whether he still had a job was beyond his capabilities right now. He called a taxi.

The chain-link fence surrounding Sparky's office building was still unlocked. It was early evening now, and Felix didn't know what kind of hours Sparky kept, but hopefully he'd still be there. He entered the dark, empty lobby and took the pitch-black elevator up to the penthouse.

As soon as he stepped off the elevator, it didn't look right. The reception desk was still there, but the switchboard and computer terminal were both gone, along with the suede cubes and the coffee table in the waiting area. No one was at the desk, so Felix cautiously ventured past it to Sparky's office.

The doors were propped wide open. Felix stood in the center of the office and looked around.

Nothing. Just a wide empty room without windows. It looked like it'd been days since Sparky had occupied this space. No desk, no chair. It was chilly and breezy in here, dark clouds rolling in outside and covering the sky.

Sparky's dumb business card was still in his pocket. Felix stared at the silly tiger logo, then dialed.

He answered on the first ring. "Omaha. What's up?" he said, before Felix had a chance to identify himself.

"You moved," Felix said. "I'm at your office, and you're not here."

"No kidding. Too many people knew where I was, no offense, and I like to keep a low profile. What can I do for you?"

"I just talked to Vish," Felix said.

"And I suppose he's been filling your head with vicious truths about me." Sparky sounded amused. "Though I imagine the Rose Princess has done a bit of that already."

"Can I talk to you?" Felix asked.

"Sure. Not on the phone, though. Stay put, I'll be there when I can." Sparky hung up.

Felix sat cross-legged on the floor of the office and stared out at the darkening skyline. He should call Jamie to see if there was any news about Michael. No. Jamie would try to talk him out of this, and now that Felix was committed to this course of action, he couldn't let anyone derail him.

It grew darker. Felix tried flipping the light switch by the door, but the power was off. He sat in shadows, staring at the dark hills on the horizon.

His phone buzzed. Jamie. He let it go to voicemail.

"Hey, Omaha." Felix turned his head. He could barely see Sparky, silhouetted in the doorway. He rose to his feet.

"Thanks for coming," he said.

Sparky walked into his office. "So what's up?"

"Help me get my brother back. Please," Felix said. "I know you said it's not the kind of thing you do, but you're the only one powerful enough to do it. You could get rid of Nicky easily if you wanted to, I know it."

"Yeah, I know it too." Sparky sounded amused. "I already said you were on your own."

"Please," Felix said again. "You make bargains with people, right? Make a bargain with me to get Michael back, and I'll do anything you want."

Sparky laughed in what seemed like genuine surprise, the sound loud in the dark room. "Omaha, that's not something a kid like you should be saying to someone like me. Where are your survival instincts?" He walked closer to Felix. "What did you think of Vish?"

"He was nice. I liked him. He told me a little bit about how he knows you."

"About why he's so mad at me, you mean?" Sparky snorted. "Yeah, I like Vish, too. And I get why he's angry and bitter, though it's probably time for him to dial it back just a bit. He's going to back me into a corner, and that's going to end badly for him, if he keeps on his current path."

"You mean *Anathema*?" Felix asked.

"Nah, *Anathema*'s great. That dude who plays me, have you seen him? He's amazing. Guy's going to win an Emmy next week. I don't think it would've killed them to go Asian for Poppy, though. Poppy's got some choice words about being played by a perky blonde." Sparky shrugged. "No, it's the prying that I have trouble with. He and his sexy detective wife are trying to find out all they can about me. Nothing good will come of that."

"It sounds like you've tried to make it up to him, whatever you did to get him so mad at you," Felix said tentatively. "I mean, he said he was a caterer before he met you, and now he's got this great life. That was nice of you."

"Nope. I did that just to mess with him. I was trying to be grateful, and he was being a pain in the ass about it, so I wanted to scare him a bit. Might've worked a little too well."

"Why'd you want me to meet him?" Felix said.

Sparky looked at him. In the darkness, his eyes glinted. "Oh, you figured that out?" he said, his tone slinky and soft. "You know that program they used to do in schools, where they introduce kids to criminals and drug addicts and take them on field trips to prisons, just to make sure they steer clear of wrong-doing in the future?"

"Yeah," Felix said. "They still do that."

"Okay, then. I figured Vish might be a good reality check for you. I thought he might be able to prevent you from doing damn fool things like telling me you'll do anything for my help." Sparky smiled, his incisors glinting in the dark. "As it turns out, I was overly optimistic."

Felix felt a quick thrill of fear. "Will you help me?" he asked.

"You don't need me," Sparky said. "The Rose Princess should be able to handle this, provided she gets her act together. Which, granted, is not a given. I'm starting to think she's a hopeless case."

"I don't know where to find Michael," Felix said. "I don't know where Nicky took him. I don't even know where to start looking."

"Stop and think about it, Omaha, instead of getting all desperate and sad," Sparky said, a touch of exasperation in his voice. "You destroyed one of them, the female demon, and she's probably just about ready to come back from her realm. She's going to need to find your brother for that, and as you've seen, they've had a few problems in the past with tracking him down. They know they've got a limited shelf life in this world, so if they're smart, they would've picked a spot for crossing back over ahead of time. The other one, your friend Nicky, he's going to bring your brother to that spot."

Felix nodded. "So where is it?" he asked.

"No idea. But Nicky has at least one human friend in the city, right?"

"Loudon Strong?"

"Our mutual friend Loudon Strong." Sparky nodded at him. "So go ask Loudon where he's hiding Nicky."

"I don't imagine he'll give me an answer," Felix said.

"He might, if you do a little strategic namedropping," Sparky said. "I'm usually not a fan of people using my name to strike terror into the hearts of their foes, but in your case I'll make an exception. But that's all I'm going to do for you."

It might be enough. "Thank you."

"Don't mention it. And Felix? Take some care."

"With Loudon?"

"With me." Sparky wasn't smiling. "I've been treading on eggshells around you, because you're a sweet kid, and nobody wants to be the guy who goes around destroying sweet kids. It's bad PR, and it's not my particular kink. Next time you call me for help, though, I'm going to make you pay up."

It took Felix a moment to nod. His heartbeat spiked, and he was newly aware of the danger in the room. "I understand," he said.

"You probably don't. But that's okay." Sparky gave him a parting salute. "Give my love to Loudon."

CHAPTER TWENTY-TWO

IT WAS ALMOST eight by the time Felix arrived at Atomic, and Loudon Strong had already left work for the day. The eighteenth floor was dark and deserted; Loudon's office doors were locked.

With a sense of resignation, Felix called another cab and gave the driver direction to Loudon's home up in the hills. If Loudon wasn't there, Felix would sit in his driveway until he returned. He could sit there all night if he had to.

It started to rain, big wet splotches that splattered against the windshield of the cab. Felix paid off the driver, then approached the intercom at the gate surrounding Loudon's home. He stabbed the button.

"What?" a male voice answered, rough and crackly through the intercom. Didn't sound like Loudon.

"Felix Dockweiler for Loudon," he said. "If he's home, tell him Sparky Mother sent me."

There was a long silence, then the gate swung open. Felix pulled the back of his shirt up over his head to protect his hair from the rain and hurried up the long driveway.

Loudon Strong stood in his front doorway. He was barefoot, in sweatpants and a t-shirt, holding what looked like Scotch in a cut crystal tumbler in one hand. He looked anxious and angry. "Did Sparky really send you?" he almost yelled.

"He told me to use his name," Felix said. Loudon flinched at that. He rocked back and forth, shifting his weight from left to right while staring at Felix with that same angry agitation. Finally, he stepped aside.

"You might as well come in," he said.

Felix entered cautiously. "Just so you know, Sparky knows I'm here," he said.

"Don't be an ass. I'm not going to do anything to you." Loudon sounded cross. "This is about your brother, I take it? He still missing?"

"I found him, but Nicky attacked me this afternoon and kidnapped him." Felix was tracking mud and water all over Loudon's inlaid wood floors. "You lied to me earlier about knowing Nicky."

"Yeah, well, I didn't exactly know Sparky was involved in this, did I?" Loudon said. "I'm sorry about your brother. You know he's probably dead, right? That's what Nicky and his girlfriend do. They burn people to death."

"Michael's alive," Felix said, and tried to believe it. "Nicky and Claire need him for their own survival. They use him to travel to this world from wherever they're from."

"Is that why they were after him? Weird." Loudon shook his head. "You want to sit?"

He gestured to a pale suede armchair. Felix shook his head. "I don't want to get your furniture wet."

Loudon exhaled, bone-deep exhaustion seeping out from beneath the worry. "Like I give a rat's ass about that right now," he said.

Felix sat. Loudon sank down on the couch facing him. He took a long drink of his Scotch. His hand shook enough to rattle the ice cubes.

"How'd you get mixed up with them?" Felix asked.

"The contracts Those goddamned contracts." Loudon almost smiled. "Nicky was hanging around outside Atomic in the early morning, waiting for you to arrive. I guess he could sense the contracts in my office. They give off some kind of . . . I don't know what they give off. Bad vibes, or something. I never should have kept them lying around. Nicky sensed them, and he came up to investigate."

Jamie's dogs had barked at Felix after he'd been to Loudon's office. Bad vibes.

"I figured right away he wasn't human. You live in L.A., after a while you get a feel for that sort of thing. What is he, anyway? Did Sparky tell you?"

"He's a fire demon," Felix said.

"Well, that makes as much sense as anything, I guess." Loudon took another drink. It seemed to steady him a little. "I like power. Everyone in this industry does, don't let them tell you otherwise. And I'm really good at finding out how to use it. I'm thirty-one, and I already run my own media conglomerate, right? So I thought Nicky might be a good resource. I offered to give him whatever help he needed." He shook his head. "Swear to you, I wasn't even thinking about the Sparky angle. It didn't occur to me until much later that this might piss him off. You're going to have to explain that to Sparky, okay?"

"What about Chad Bryson?" Loudon looked blank, so Felix elaborated. "The intern. Did you know that Nicky killed him?"

"Of course. He did it in front of me. I wanted a demonstration of his power. I didn't know he'd take it that far, but it sure was effective," Loudon said. "Is Sparky mad about that?"

"Chad worked in entertainment, so yeah, Sparky's mad," Felix said.

"Shit. Didn't think of that," Loudon said. He sat back in his chair and thought for a bit. "They're at my house, the new one I'm building in Malibu, Nicky and that woman. I've been letting them crash there while it's under construction. Tell Sparky that they're there. And then you tell Sparky I was helpful to you, okay? Tell him I didn't know Nicky was going to kill anyone. You know what, tell him I was trying to keep them in one spot so he could deal with them."

"Thanks for letting me know," Felix said. He got to his feet. Loudon rose as well and stopped him with a hand on his arm.

"Get me off the hook with Sparky, and you can write your own job description at Atomic. You want to host your own show, you can host your own show. If I come out of this alive and with my job intact and with Sparky still cool with me, I will have your back forever, Felix."

"You let Nicky kill one of your employees, and you didn't even remember his name," Felix said.

"He wasn't an employee, he was an *intern*," Loudon said. "Don't screw things up for both of us just because you're feeling butthurt about some dead intern."

Felix stared at him, unable to come up with a suitable reply.

Gretchen and Heidi were lying down in the living room, flanking either side of the front door like a pair of canine sphinxes, when he finally returned to the duplex. One of them growled at Felix—probably smelling something funny on him, which wasn't surprising, considering all the dark places he'd visited during his long and terrible day—but Jamie snapped at her, and she quieted down.

"Where've you been?" Jamie asked. He sat on the couch, with Young sitting on the floor in front of him, leaning her back against his legs. It was a companionable pose, almost intimate, but they both looked tense and exhausted. Young nodded at Felix in greeting, but said nothing. "Have you been talking to the police all this time?"

"Michael is at London Strong's unfinished Malibu home. He gave me the address," Felix said. "Nicky's been hiding out there."

"Wait. What? How do you know this?" Jamie asked. "I doubt Strong volunteered that information."

"He did, actually. I gave him the proper incentive to tell me the truth." Felix sat down in an armchair. His legs felt tired, so tired. Felt like he might never stand up again.

Jamie looked confused. Before he could say anything, Young spoke. "He went to see Sparky again." Her tone was sharp.

"Did you?" Jamie's eyes widened.

"Let's find Michael first. You can get mad at me about that later," Felix said. "Young, Sparky said you have the ability to handle Nicky and Claire on your own. He was pretty adamant about that."

"News to me," Young said.

"That's what he said. He implied it would be no big deal."

Jamie leaned forward. "So Sparky's not going to help us?"

Felix shook his head. "I asked him. He said no."

"Good." Jamie flopped back on the couch, his shoulders boneless with visible relief. "That's the only positive thing I've heard all day."

"Will you go with me to Malibu, Young?" Felix asked. "I know you said you don't know how to do anything, but . . ."

"If I can do something, I will. At least I'll give it a try," Young said.

She looked exhausted and frustrated. Behind her on the couch, Jamie's expression mirrored hers. Felix knew the feeling.

CHAPTER TWENTY-THREE

THEY LEFT IN the wee hours of the morning, while it was still dark outside. A curtain of rain pounded down on the windshield of Jamie's hybrid during the drive to Malibu. The interior of the car was foggy and damp and smelled of wet dog; Gretchen and Heidi warred with Felix for room to sprawl out in the tiny backseat.

Young rode up front with Jamie. At first she'd refused to get in the car, volunteering instead to take a bus and meet them there. Jamie had pointed out that buses didn't run with any kind of frequency at this early hour, and time was of the essence. She'd seen the logic in that, but she was visibly uncomfortable. Her good hand repeatedly clutched and released the shoulder strap of her seatbelt.

Jamie had suggested Felix stay behind. The clear implication was he'd be more of a hindrance than a help, which made him feel miserable and snubbed. He felt guilty, too, because he was almost incapacitated with fear at the thought of what they were going to do, and a significant part of him desperately wanted to take Jamie up on his suggestion. Then he thought about what Michael must be suffering at the hands of Nicky—what Michael had already suffered—and he knew he had no business chickening out.

Loudon's unfinished home was situated on a high sandy cliff above the ocean. A plywood fence, its door secured with a thick chain and a padlock, encircled the entire construction site. Jamie parked on the road and stood in the rain outside the fence. He examined the lock, then popped his trunk and rummaged around in his toolbox for a heavy pair of bolt cutters. A grunt and a snip, and the padlock fell open.

Jamie passed the bolt cutters to Felix. "Here," he said. "You said Claire's skin tore easily, right?"

"Nicky's, too, when I gouged him with my keys," Felix said.

"If they get near you, hit them with these and try to burst the skin. Then get the hell out of the way so you don't get burned." He rooted around in his toolbox. "Young?"

"I've got this." She hoisted her cane.

"Great. If we hit them fast, this might be easy. Especially if the ladies do some of the hard work for us." Jamie selected a long-handled ball peen hammer for himself, then closed the trunk. He let the dogs out of the backseat. They swarmed around his legs, snorfling and whining. "Hush," he told them. "You're going to want to make noise, I know, but try to be as quiet as you can right now."

He didn't bother with their leashes. He held onto the collar of one dog, and the other stayed close to his opposite side. He glanced at Felix and Young. "Ready?"

Young nodded once. Felix swallowed and nodded as well.

They walked up the driveway to the house. The house was big and modern, with dark gray walls made from what looked like interlocking slabs of shale. Huge picture windows faced the driveway. The darkness and the rain would provide some cover for their approach, but if Nicky happened to look outside. . .

Jamie touched Felix's shoulder and pointed at the house. Felix looked through the windows and saw it, too. A glowing fire.

Jamie tried the front door. Locked. He glanced at Felix and Young, then stepped back, rolled his shoulders, raised one booted foot, and kicked the door just beneath the knob.

It flew open with a bang. Jamie gave each dog a quick pat on the head. "Go!" he yelled.

Gretchen and Heidi flew through the door into the darkness, transforming seamlessly from domesticated pets into feral creatures hunting down their prey. Their barks and howls echoed around the empty entryway.

Hammer in hand, Jamie took off after them. Young clutched her cane and followed at a slower pace. Felix stayed close to her.

Just beyond the foyer was the living room, unfinished and unfurnished. Felix smelled fresh paint and wood smoke.

Michael, his wrists bound with rope, dangled from a ceiling hook in front of the lit fireplace. He was shirtless, and his head drooped. The circular burn on his chest seemed larger and was now an angry, blistered red. He wasn't moving.

Nicky burst into the living room from the back of the house. He looked confused and alarmed by the ruckus. His eyes widened as they met Felix's. "What are—"

The dogs were on him before he had a chance to finish the question. One sank her teeth into his thigh, while the other jumped up and tore at his throat. Orange flames leapt out from inside the ripped flesh.

"Now!" Jamie rushed toward Nicky and swung his hammer in a wide arc. Nicky lurched back to avoid the blow, but the hammer caught his shoulder. He fell to the floorboards, the dogs on top of him.

Fire consumed Nicky. The dogs scurried back, whimpering as the flames grew too hot for them to continue their attack. Her cane at the ready, Young hovered just beside Jamie, ready to strike if Nicky tried to get to his feet. From the floor, Nicky screeched and flailed. In the air was an acrid chemical stench, like burned plastic.

While Jamie and Young were occupied with Nicky, Felix hurried over to Michael. He wasn't tall enough to reach Michael's tied hands, and there was no furniture in the room, so he ignored his bonds for the moment and focused on determining whether he was still alive.

"Michael? It's Felix. You're safe now," he said. Michael made a small incoherent murmur in reply. His eyes were still closed, but his drooping head raised a bit.

An arm snaked around Felix's throat. "Sorry, darling, but I'm afraid you can't have him," Claire said in his ear. "Nicky and I are going to need your baby brother for a good long time."

She must've been in the back of the house. Her arm was hot against his skin. Felix pulled out of her grasp and turned to face her.

She was whole and looked human, even though the last time he'd seen her she'd been nothing more than a melted splotch on the ground. "You resurrected," he said.

"That's the wrong word. 'Resurrect' implies death and re-birth, neither of which apply to me. Michael doesn't give us life. He just provides us with a means of transportation from our home to yours," she said. She winked at him. "Nicky said he bashed in your pretty face, darling. I'm delighted to see he was exaggerating."

One of the dogs jumped at her. She raised one hand, fingers spread, her palm glowing red. Before the dog could bite, she grabbed it by the muzzle and squeezed hard.

The dog made a high-pitched whine and struggled out of Claire's fiery grasp before slinking back to the far wall, whimpering softly. Felix smelled singed hair and charred flesh.

Claire smiled at Felix. "In the long term, this isn't a fight you can win," she said. "We might not last long, but Nicky and I can keep coming back here, forever and ever, and there's no way Michael can hide from us."

"Then I'll keep protecting him, as many times as it takes," Felix said. His voice shook. He clutched the bolt cutters Jamie had given him, ready to wield them as a weapon if Claire moved toward him.

"You can't protect him if you're dead," she said. "You know I have a soft spot for you, but you and your friends are in the way."

"Don't waste time talking to her, Felix," Jamie said. "Either hit her, or get out of here."

"Jamie." Young's tone held a clear warning note. Jamie and Felix turned to see the fiery, lumpy, melting mass that was Nicky start to writhe and pulse.

Even as Felix watched, sickened and scared, Nicky's flesh healed. The strange, stretchy skin pulled back into place, once again containing the flames inside his body. At first he looked grotesquely misshapen, then he gradually shifted back into his former shape. He rose to his feet, his clothes in burned tatters on his body, and stretched his arms over his head as though making sure his muscles still worked.

"Close, kids, but not close enough," he said. His gaze fell on Felix. His eyes narrowed. "Last time I saw you, you were more dead than alive. I could have sworn I broke your jaw."

Felix had to swallow hard before he spoke. "I have friends in high places," he said. He was pleased with how it came out. It had a nice air of bravado to it.

"Yeah? I don't see them anywhere," Nicky said.

"Look around you. You're outnumbered," Jamie said.

"So what?" Nicky replied. "Like that even matters. You defeat us now, we'll keep coming back, again and again and again."

"Then I guess we'll have to keep defeating you, won't we?" Jamie said. He raised the ball peen hammer to his shoulder like a baseball bat.

"Go ahead. Destroy us, we come back, repeat as necessary. How long do you think you can keep that up before we get the upper hand and burn you to death?" Nicky asked. "I mean, you could always kill little Michael over there, and that would probably keep us out of your backyard for good, but I don't see any of you jumping at that option."

"Probably not. But I assure you, it's been considered." It was a woman's voice, clear and confident. Everyone turned to look at the new arrival.

Poppy Kang posed in the entrance to the foyer. She wore a short belted cherry-red trench coat with a draping hood, which she pushed back to reveal her shiny bob of copper hair. Her makeup was immaculate. Knee-high spike-heeled boots in shiny black patent leather clicked on the floorboards as she strolled into the living room.

"I thought I'd see how Young was coming along," she said. She looked around the room, at Nicky in his semi-charred near-naked glory, at Claire's glowing hand, at Young and Jamie, at the

194

whimpering dogs, at Michael, bound and unconscious. She shook her head. "This is messy and disappointing."

"Who the hell are you supposed to be?" Nicky asked.

She ignored him. "Felix, come over here for a second. There's something I want to give you."

"Stay where you are," Claire said to him. She held out her hand in clear warning, her palm glowing orange.

Poppy looked at her. There was something calm and curious about her expression. In the light from the fireplace, her eyes seemed to softly glow. "I don't need to hear from you," she said. "Felix?"

Felix walked over to her. His legs felt light and unsteady. She smiled at him, gentle and reassuring. For the first time, he noticed she had dimples. "Don't take this the wrong way," she said.

She reached out with one slender hand, grabbed his chin, leaned forward, and kissed him.

She tasted of oranges and espresso. Felix was too stunned to either pull back or respond, so he stayed motionless until she released his chin and stepped back. "There," she said.

"What was that for?" Felix asked. It was a little breathless.

"Turn around and tell me what you see," she said.

He turned around, and the world changed.

CHAPTER TWENTY-FOUR

HE WAS SILENT. From behind him, Poppy placed her hands on his shoulders and leaned in, her lips close to his ear. "What do you see, Felix?" she asked again.

He shook his head. "Nothing," he said.

"Nothing?"

"Nothing. It's like I've gone blind, but . . ."

"But what?" Poppy sounded amused. Felix just shook his head again.

"Your eyes are working fine. Your brain is just having a little trouble processing what your eyes are telling you." Her voice was reassuring in his ear. "Keep looking."

He stared at the room. Details began to fall into place: There was Jamie with his hammer, looking at him in what seemed to be horror, and there was one of the dogs, the burned one, lying on the ground with its muzzle down and its front paws splayed to either side, and there was the other dog, prowling around Nicky.

He felt like vomiting. Pain grew behind his eyes, a pressure that spread throughout his brain, like something was going to explode very soon if he didn't look away. Poppy rubbed his shoulders. "Look at Young," she said. "Look at Young, and tell her what you see."

He couldn't see Young at all, and then the pressure in his head shifted a little, and he realized he was staring right at her. She took a step toward him, frowning as though something beyond her comprehension was taking place.

Her face was smooth and unscarred, her now-undamaged right eye symmetrical with her left. Her cane . . . Felix *really* couldn't look directly at her cane, because it flickered in and out of his vision, glowing and pulsing, and his head throbbed in violent surges of pain with each pulse.

"Young," he said. His voice sounded odd and foreign to his ears. "Hold your cane in your other hand."

Young went still, gazing at him with a blank expression. Her arm, the arm that didn't exist, twitched.

She raised her new arm in front of her face and stared at it for a moment. Then she shifted her cane to her right hand.

The room filled with a dark gray light, phosphorescent and terrifying. The light brought sounds that Felix couldn't identify, a cacophony that filled the room, like millions of hushed voices whispering at once.

Black fire. That was how Felix's brain resolved the images of Claire and Nicky now, black fire, even though he knew that wasn't really what he was seeing, that his brain was simply trying to translate the images into a form it could understand. Claire and Nicky were twin animate beings of black fire, and as Felix watched and tried to make sense of it, Young sliced the glowing spike that used to be her cane through the gray light and, with the slightest touch to each, extinguished both fires.

The phosphorescent gray light went out along with the twin black fires. In the glow from the fireplace, Young was her usual damaged self once again. Her cane clattered uselessly to the floorboards.

The scent of wet smoke was heavy in the room, laced with a pungent stench of sulfur. From behind Felix, Poppy patted his shoulder.

"They'll keep using Michael to come back, unless you destroy them for good this time," she said. "Be a doll and rip out their hearts."

Claire and Nicky lay sprawled on the floor, lifeless, neither moving nor burning, as though Young's attack had frozen them in some strange in-between state. They were still in human form, or something close to it. They looked like melting wax mannequins.

Rip out their hearts. It was impossible to even think of doing that, and yet as Felix stared at them, his vision underwent another shift, and Claire and Nicky changed again. Now they looked like human-shaped plastic sacks of tar, black and shiny. Something glowed from deep within the tar, matching pinpoints of black light.

He glanced back at Poppy, seeking reassurance that this was indeed what he should do, and recoiled as his optic nerves sent another faulty message to his brain.

He faced forward, then knelt between Claire and Nicky. He set down the bolt cutters. Jamie said something to him, his voice loud and angry, but Felix's ears weren't working right anymore, either, and in any case, Jamie's protests didn't seem important.

He stretched out both arms and laid a hand on each bag of tar. They felt warm and rubbery and faintly sticky to the touch.

He pushed. The bags ruptured, and now his wrists were submerged in warm black tar. There were no bones, nothing to impede his progress as he groped around in the tar, until each hand closed around something hard and small.

He rose to his feet, his movements slow and languid. It felt like his body no longer belonged to him, like he was somewhere far away, safe in bed maybe, watching the remnants of a fading dream in the seconds before waking.

"Give them to me," Poppy said, her voice gentle. She reached out a hand.

Felix carefully placed the small hard objects—the hearts—into her palm. His hands and sleeves were clean, he noted vaguely, with no sign of the sticky black substance anywhere on them.

The hearts were black and round. They glittered in the light from the fireplace. Poppy smiled at him. "Thank you." She slipped them into the pocket of her trench coat.

And with that, the pressure in his head ebbed, and the urge to vomit receded. His vision and his hearing both fully returned to normal. He looked down at Nicky and Claire, who now were just sticky melted patches of plasticky goop on the floorboards.

Young looked grim; Jamie looked horrified. "What the hell was that, Felix?" he asked.

Felix started to answer, then stopped as another, more pressing thought came to him. "Michael!"

The construction workers had left a sturdy metal stepladder in the uncompleted kitchen. Felix used it to climb up and untie Michael's hands; Jamie helped lower him to the ground. "He's breathing," Jamie said. His face was tense.

"He should be fine. He's been through this several times before, after all," Poppy said. "Not that it hasn't been deeply traumatic for him, but he'll recover. Best of all, it'll never happen again."

She nodded at Young. "Have you figured it out yet?"

"I suppose so," Young said. She seemed stunned and unsteady. "Thank you."

"No problem. I thought you might want a little push in the right direction."

Poppy crouched in front of the injured dog. The dog growled and snapped at her, but seemed too weak to attack. "Knock it off. I know you don't like me, but in this case, I'm here to help," Poppy said. The dog continued to growl as Poppy placed her hands on either side of its burned muzzle. Jamie took a step forward, ready to intervene if necessary.

She rose to her feet and straightened out the hem of her coat. "She'll be fine. She's been a good girl," she said to Jamie.

Young's eyes narrowed. "Poppy, I know you can't heal things," she said.

"No?" Poppy raised a flawless eyebrow. Her pert nose wrinkled. "It smells disgusting in here. Let's take this outside, shall we?"

"Help me with Michael," Felix said to Jamie. Between the two of them, they managed to get Michael to his feet and carry him outside. Michael made a soft moan and his eyelids fluttered, but he still didn't wake up.

They walked down the driveway. The rain had slowed to a drizzle, and the sky had lightened. Poppy nodded at what was presumably her vehicle, a sleek black sports car. "I think that's everything I can do here."

"Thanks for helping us," Felix said as she climbed into the driver's seat. She flashed him her dimples again and waved at him. Jamie and Young were silent, their expressions grim.

It looked like there was maybe someone sitting in the passenger seat, but Poppy's windows were tinted, and Felix couldn't tell for sure.

Jamie watched after her as she drove off, then gave what seemed like an involuntary shudder. "Let's get the hell out of this place," he said.

"I'm walking," Young said.

"Really? It's six in the morning, and downtown is like thirty miles from here."

She shook her head. "I need to walk," she said. With a final nod at Felix and Jamie, she started down the road.

Jamie looked frustrated and unhappy. "Crap," he said. "Felix, is everything okay with you?"

"I think so. Maybe. When all that was happening, what did you see?"

Jamie just shook his head. "Let's go home," he said.

CHAPTER TWENTY-FIVE

FELIX ACCOMPANIED MICHAEL to the security checkpoint at LAX. He felt a tightness in his chest, a reluctance to let his brother out of his sight.

"We could drive, you know," he said. It wasn't the first time he'd made the suggestion. "Cancel your ticket, and we'll do a road trip to Chicago. It'd be fun. It's not like I have anything more pressing going on right now."

Michael smiled. "Don't be stupid," he said. "I don't have time for a road trip. Classes start Monday, and I still need to move into campus housing." He rummaged in his backpack and produced his plane ticket and identification.

"Yeah, but after everything that happened . . ." Felix exhaled. "I feel like there's more we need to discuss. A lot more."

"Like figuring out whether my real dad was a fire demon?" Michael gave him a sour grin. "Yeah. Maybe we'll spring that one on mom at Christmas. You're coming home, aren't you?"

"Sure, yeah," Felix said. "Maybe I'll visit you on campus before that."

Michael nodded. "You sure they're gone forever?" It was a little too deliberately nonchalant.

"They're not coming back," Felix said.

"Well." There was more they needed to say, much more, but it probably wouldn't get said even during the prolonged intimacy of a cross-country road trip, much less in a crowded airport, so Felix kept silent and just hugged his brother. Michael buried his face in his neck and clutched him like he'd never let go.

Felix hung back and watched as Michael made his way through a very long and very slow line to the security checkpoint. After Michael had finally disappeared from view, he returned to his car in the short-term parking structure, climbed in the front seat, buried his head in his arms on the steering wheel, and sobbed.

They were installing the baseboards, crisp and bright white against the deep blue walls of Jamie's restaurant. They worked in silence. Gretchen and Heidi sprawled in front of the open door, alert for any visitors.

They hadn't talked much in the last few days, and that was probably for the best. There was too much Felix couldn't put into words. Whatever questions Jamie had raised about what had gone down at Loudon Strong's Malibu house had gone unanswered.

"So Young left me," Jamie said, breaking the silence.

Felix put down his hammer and looked at him in surprise. "What?"

Jamie shrugged. "She said she had to figure out what she's becoming." He shook his head. "I get it. She's got a lot to deal with, and I'm a distraction."

Felix paused. "She's not human, is she?"

"I don't know. I doubt if she knows," Jamie said. "It's like she told us earlier. She died once, and not all of her came back. Part of her exists somewhere else."

"Are you okay with it? Her leaving you, I mean?"

Another shrug. "On the one hand, maybe it'll be nice getting back to normal. I got enough in my life right now with the band and the restaurant and my properties, it's not like I needed all that supernatural crap on top of that."

"It still sucks, though," Felix said.

"That it does, my friend."

They continued on, working in silence until the shadows grew long and the sky grew dark and it was time to return to the duplex.

Felix's last day at Atomic was anticlimactic. They gave him a banker's box to hold all his personal belongings, but he'd never personalized the cubicle he shared with Jenny, so all it held was a notepad and a *Meltdown!* coffee mug, which rolled around in the bottom of the box as he carried it to the elevator. Just before he left, Jenny slipped her arm around his shoulders and gave him a squeeze, genuinely distressed that her success necessitated his failure.

The news that Jenny had been awarded the permanent staff position had been overshadowed by the minor bombshell that Tasha's contract hadn't been renewed. Her last day was the same as Felix's. Everyone in the newsroom was busy preparing for coverage of the upcoming Emmy Awards, so there was no formal farewell party. They ended up taking the elevator out of the building together, Felix with his almost-empty box, Tasha with her rolling leather briefcase. She looked at his box and almost smiled.

"They're packing up my office and shipping everything to me later," she said.

He stared at her for a moment as a fragment of a memory flickered through his brain. There was something he'd meant to tell her, something about the reason why her contract hadn't been renewed, but he couldn't quite remember what it was. Probably wasn't anything important.

The elevator doors opened into the lobby. She nodded at him as she stepped out. "Good luck in all you do, Felix."

Outside the building, it was hot and blindingly bright. The midday sun reflected off the white pavement. Last week's rain was a distant memory.

On the low cement wall surrounding the building, the same wall that Young Park had sat beside while watching over Felix during his strange night meeting with Loudon Strong, perched a familiar figure. Felix stared at Sparky for a moment, then walked over to him.

Today, Sparky was comparatively casual in a crisp white shirt unbuttoned at the collar. Pinstriped trousers, tasseled black loafers, a wide gold watch on his tanned wrist. He smiled at Felix and removed his gold-rimmed sunglasses. "Take a seat, Omaha," he said.

"Are you here to see me?" Felix asked.

It was both a relief and a disappointment when Sparky shook his head. "Nope. I've got a meeting with our good friend Loudon in a few minutes. I thought if I timed it right, I might be able to catch you on your walk of shame."

"Do I owe you anything?" Felix asked. "For helping out with Nicky and Claire?"

Another headshake. "That was all Poppy. She and the Rose Princess were tight, once upon a whenever, so she felt personally invested."

It sounded plausible, but Felix still wondered. Sparky looked at him, a half-grin playing on his lips. "What?"

"Nothing. Just . . ." Felix swallowed hard, then decided to say it. "I guess I'm wondering if you'd taste like oranges and coffee if I kissed you."

Sparky burst out laughing in what seemed like startled delight. "Is that what Poppy tastes like? I wouldn't actually know." He considered. "Okay, I might have been there in spirit, as it were. But it was Poppy's suggestion. I have a hard time turning that woman down. When did you figure it out?"

"The dog. It was burned pretty badly. Young said Poppy can't heal things, and I know you can. And also . . ." He stopped.

"What?"

"When I was seeing things funny. When I saw what Young and Claire and Nicky really looked like, I couldn't see Poppy." He sought for a way to explain it. "I'd look at her, and my brain would scream at me not to really *see* her."

"Give your brain a bit of credit for that one. That's an excellent piece of self-preservation." Sparky looked amused. "Yeah, there are times when it might not be entirely wise to look directly at me. That was one of those times."

"What are you going to do about Loudon?" Felix asked.

"I haven't decided yet. I thought I'd play it by ear, see how the meeting goes," Sparky said.

"He asked me to put in a good word for him with you," Felix said.

"Is that what you're doing?" Sparky asked. It seemed like the answer mattered to him.

Felix shook his head. "He didn't care that Nicky killed Chad Bryson. It might've been Loudon's idea, actually. He asked for a demonstration of his powers."

Sparky nodded, digesting this. His expression suddenly brightened. "Oh, hey, I got you a souvenir." He reached into his

206

pocket and extracted a small jeweler's case covered in bottle-green velvet. He passed it to Felix. Startled, Felix opened it.

Cufflinks. Glittery black rocks fashioned into matching baby tigers, mounted on gold. Felix stared at Sparky. "Are these . . . ?"

"Their hearts. You bet. I thought you might want something to commemorate your moment of badassness. You ripped the hearts out of a pair of fire demons, Omaha."

"Thank you," Felix said. His voice sounded a little strained.

"Don't mention it." Sparky leaned back and squinted into the sun. "So you're unemployed now, huh?"

Felix felt a sudden wary tremor. "Uh-huh."

"You should call Vish," Sparky said. "He might write you a part in his show. You can play the sweet-faced kid from the Midwest who falls under the malevolent spell of Carlos Mater."

Felix had no idea what to say to that. Sparky rose to his feet and clapped him on the shoulder. "I'm pretty damn sure our paths will cross again, Omaha."

Without looking back at Felix, he sauntered into the building. Felix remained in one place on the wall for a very long time, staring at the cufflinks.

Interested in discovering more about Sparky Mother? Here's a peek at the first chapters of Morgan Richter's *Wrong City*, the suspenseful prequel to *Demon City*. *Wrong City* is available in paperback and as an ebook from Luft Books.

CHAPTER ONE

THE PARTY WAS already on the decline when the girl in the bumblebee dress climbed onto the patio railing. Silhouetted by the Los Angeles skyline, which crawled along the horizon in an unbroken stretch of glittery lights, she stood on the slim beam and wobbled.

Vish watched her, his hands clutching his near-depleted bamboo tray of bite-sized chimichangas. She shouldn't be doing that. One wrong step, one wobble too far, and this girl, whoever she was, would tumble into the darkness of the canyon below, gone forever. Vish couldn't see anything beyond the reach of the lamps at the edge of the patio; where their light ended, blackness began and swept down the hillside, stopped only by the barricade of sparkly lights that marked Hollywood Boulevard.

There were murmurs from the guests: amusement, disapproval, no overt concern. The girl shifted sideways, one tiny foot in front of the other on the railing, arms raised at her sides, poised like a gymnast preparing to execute a flip.

Not that a gymnast would wear those shoes. They were shiny leather—the stark light from the lamps drained color from everything it touched, so Vish couldn't be sure, but he thought they were bright blue—with pointy toes and skinny gold spikes for heels. She wasn't really dressed as a bumblebee, not literally, but that'd been Vish's immediate thought upon seeing her. Her dress was short and strapless, made from a narrow length of ruffled yellow taffeta wrapped around and around her tiny body until her waist looked wider than her slight shoulders. A black fringe dangled from the ruffle, giving the impression of horizontal stripes that shifted and rippled as she moved. It was belted with a wide black satin sash, the ends of which spilled down to her ankles. She could trip on them, lose her balance, fall to her death.

Someone should stop her. He should stop her. Vish hovered near the patio door.

"Better watch your step, Kels," a woman called out from the crowd. She laughed, teeth glinting in the patio lights. Her face glistened with perspiration, and to Vish's eyes she looked slithery and unearthly, a golem calling for the blood of this girl.

The girl—Kels?—shook her head. She had a mess of pale hair, cut short and jagged, which stuck up like a cloud of downy fluff around her head. She was very pretty, in a childlike way, and she seemed much too young to be at this party, amongst this collection of directors and producers and sundry members of the entertainment industry. The bulk of the guests were in their forties or beyond, Vish guessed, though it was hard to be certain with all the lean, toned bodies and tight, unlined skin on display.

"I'm fine," the girl said. Her voice was light and babyish. "Look, I'm perfectly balanced." She pivoted on the railing, pointed toes shifting smartly, until she faced the guests. "I could do a cartwheel on here."

She seemed sober, at least. Clear eyes, no flushed skin, no slurred speech. Still, Vish felt his stomach clench in anticipation of something terrible. Should he step in and haul her down from there? Should he find the hostess and alert her to the possible tragedy and/or lawsuit waiting to happen on her patio?

The girl glanced over her pale shoulder. "I can't even see the bottom," she said. "If I fell, they'd have to wait until morning to look for me."

A man angled through the assembled guests and approached the railing. Laughing, he held a hand up to her. "Time to come down, darling," he said.

The girl smiled. She had a dimple in each cheek. She crouched and took his hand in her own dainty one, then hopped down to the patio floor. She wobbled on the gold spikes when she landed, but she stayed upright.

Vish's stomach relaxed. His face felt hot. Silly to get so worked up; she was fine. She'd been fine all along, she was having a good time, and he was an overprotective ninny. It was just the combination of the crowd, and the looming blackness beyond the patio, and maybe something in the night air that made him feel anxious.

The girl tilted her face up and pecked the man on his jaw. "You always take such good care of me," she said.

Huh. The man was probably in his early thirties, a few years older than Vish, and thus was too old to be her date. He was pretty, slim and foxlike, with glossy black hair worn long in front, short in back. Dark eyes, a mad fringe of black eyelashes, dark golden skin.

The man murmured something to the girl that Vish couldn't hear. She giggled in reply, then released him and drifted off into the crowd.

So they weren't a couple, or probably weren't. Vish looked at the man, aware of the combination of gratitude and envy he felt for the easy way he took charge of the situation. He wore what was almost certainly a terribly expensive suit, with sleek lines and a burnished shimmer to the fabric. He didn't look familiar exactly, but he looked like someone Vish should know, like his life would be richer and more interesting for including him in his circle of acquaintances.

He was here to work, not to ogle the guests. His sad little tray of chimichangas was cold. He entered through the open French doors into the heart of the party.

He skidded on the floor, which was made of raised, rounded tiles, polished until they gleamed. In his best shoes, Vish could barely walk without wobbling or sliding. From behind him, a hand clamped around his upper arm, holding him in place.

He glanced back at his assailant, a fierce, compact woman in a sleeveless batik-patterned dress that displayed her ropy biceps to full effect. It was the hostess, Maryanne something-or-other, and she looked furious. Her grip on Vish's arm tightened; her thin lips twisted into a snarl.

She didn't look at him. Her attention was fixed on the far end of the living room where Jamie, her own empty tray held by her side, was cornered by a middle-aged man with a tidy beard.

Ah. Maryanne's husband. Jamie had pointed him out to Vish and Toby while they were loading their trays in the kitchen earlier.

"She's supposed to be serving guests, not schmoozing," Maryanne said. Her forehead creased, her sculpted eyebrows almost touching. "It's unprofessional."

If Jamie was schmoozing, she was doing a poor job of it. The man carried on what appeared to be a lively monologue while Jamie nodded at frequent intervals, her blonde ponytail bobbing up and down. Her expression showed nothing but polite interest, but she seemed to be recoiling from him, pressing herself against the sofa in the hopes it would swallow her up.

"Every time I've looked at her, she's been gabbing with my husband. This isn't a networking event for the caterers. She's not going to get cast in one of his films just because she served him a taco."

Vish cleared his throat. "You know, I really don't think she's trying—"

"I don't want to get her in trouble, but I'm a step away from going into the kitchen and telling her boss."

Vish paused. The only one in the kitchen was Toby, and the idea of Toby as anyone's boss seemed ludicrous. "Ah… she's in charge. She owns the company."

Maryanne looked at him for the first time. The forehead crease deepened. Vish hastened to continue. "I'll pass your concerns along to her."

"Do that." Maryanne shifted her attention back to Jamie. "She's an actress, isn't she?"

"She does this full-time now."

"But she used to act, didn't she? She's got that actressy look." The snarl relaxed into a contemptuous smirk. "It's a cliché because it's true: Everyone in the service industry in this town is a wannabe movie star."

Vish smiled. "I'm not," he said.

Maryanne glanced at him again. She looked puzzled. "No, of course you're not," she said. Like she was explaining something obvious to someone who had difficulty with simple concepts.

Vish took a moment to sort that one out. Maryanne pointed her chin at Jamie. "Talk to her. I spend a lot of money on my parties, and my friends value my recommendations. Right now, I don't think I have much good to say about you people."

Vish nodded. "Sure. Of course. No problem."

Maryanne looked unappeased. She maintained her death-grip on his arm. It hurt. At a loss for a graceful way to free himself, he proffered his tray. "Chimichanga?"

Success. She released him. One hand hovered above the tray, then she hesitated. "Those are eggrolls?" she asked.

"Chimichangas. Like little deep-fried burritos," Vish said.

She grimaced and shook her head. "I don't eat anything fried." The hand withdrew. She stalked off, expertly navigating the rounded tiles in her spike-heeled sandals.

At a low chuckle behind him, Vish turned. Ah. The pretty man from the patio. "No, of course you're not an actor," the man said in a perfect imitation of Maryanne. "Whatever do you suppose she meant by that?"

Vish smiled. "I'm sure it wasn't flattering," he said. "I imagine she was saying I'm insufficiently cute to be a movie star."

"Says her," the man said. He winked. "Could be simple bias, you know. She could be saying you're insufficiently white to be a movie star."

His tone was casual, almost flippant. The man was nearly as dark as Vish, though it was tough to pinpoint his ethnic background. Latino? Filipino? Neither seemed quite right.

No way was Vish was going to be lured into chatting about the party's hostess while standing in the middle of her living room, surrounded by her guests. He held up his tray. "Chimichanga?"

The man glanced at the offering on display. "God, no," he said. He waggled his empty glass. "Can you get me a refill, or do I fetch it myself?"

Jamie didn't have a liquor license. Maryanne had hired the bartender separately, and the libations didn't fall into Vish's territory. He took the glass from the man. "I can get it. What are you having?"

"Scotch. Dude at the bar will know what. Thanks."

The bar was set up in the sunken dining room, through a narrow archway bordered with hand-painted ceramic tiles. "I need a Scotch," Vish said to the bartender, a sullen kid with hair winched back into a low ponytail.

The kid looked skeptical. Vish shook his head. "Not for me. For that guy," he said. He pointed through the arch in the direction of the pretty man. "He said you'd know what he was drinking."

The bartender scowled. "Him. Yeah." He fingered his way through a selection of bottles atop the rolling cart that served as a portable bar, picked one, and tossed a few cubes into a fresh glass. "Rocks, water, right?"

"I have no idea."

The bartender shrugged, fixed the drink, and handed over the glass. "Here you go."

"Thanks. Do you know who he is? That man?"

"Never seen him before, but everyone here is acting like he's the shit. Probably a studio exec or whatever. He's got a stupid name, Stubby or Stumpy or something."

The pretty man didn't look like a Stubby, or a Stumpy. Vish glanced at him again. He was now at the center of a small throng, deep in conversation with a cluster of party guests, the girl in the bumblebee dress among them. She snaked her arm up his back and hooked her hand over his shoulder, her body curving into his. He seemed unaware of her presence, his attention fixed on the bearded host. Good to see Jamie had finally escaped his clutches.

"Open calls only sound like a good idea, but they're more hassle than they're worth," the host was saying. "I found this great kid last month—good-looking guy, theater background, an absolute nobody but perfect for the part, so I took a gamble and cast him. A week into shooting, he disappears on me. Doesn't show up at his call time, doesn't answer his phone. I sent a PA over to his apartment to pound on his door, but no dice. We're going to have to recast ASAP."

"Rough break," the pretty man said.

"You're telling me. Now there's a whole list of re-shoots I've got to get through, all because the kid turned out to be a goddamned flake." He chuckled. "Of course, if it turns out he died or something, I'm going to sound like a real douche here, right?"

The pretty man nodded. "Been hearing a lot of that these days. I mean actors disappearing, not you sounding like a douche. Seems to be an epidemic." He reached out and accepted his drink from Vish. "Thanks, man," he said. A smile and another wink. Friendly. Flirtatious, maybe. Hard to tell.

Vish smiled back and withdrew.

The chimichangas looked sadder than ever. He headed into the kitchen, which was connected through another archway, one step down from the dining room, which itself was a step down from the living room. Between the slick tiles and the steps in unexpected places, someone was going to trip over his feet and break his neck before the end of the night. That someone would probably be Vish.

In the kitchen, Jamie reloaded her tray with hot hors d'oeuvres. She dumped a handful of crumbled Manchego over pumpkin empanadas, their flaky crusts brown from the oven. "There. That should prevent confusion, right?" she asked. "I've

216

had two guests complain that they thought these would be sweet, like miniature pumpkin pies. The pork in the filling really threw them off." She glanced up at Vish. "Everything going okay out there?"

"Fine," he said. He paused. "Maryanne saw you talking to her husband." He made it as light as possible.

Jamie looked at him. Her expression sharpened. She nodded once. "Ah," she said. "How are the chimichangas going over?"

"Hard to say," he said. "Eggrolls are fried, right?"

"Of course. Why?"

Vish shrugged. "Just asking."

Toby hauled a hot cookie sheet out of the oven and plunked it down on the tile counter. Jamie hurried to maneuver a potholder beneath it. The sheet held an array of miniature chicken tacos, the corn tortillas translucent with hot grease. "Hey, did you see Kelsey?" Toby asked.

"Who?"

Both Toby and Jamie turned to stare at him. "Kelsey Kirkpatrick," Jamie said, the incredulity plain in her voice. "From *Interstellar Boys*?"

Vish shook his head. "I don't have a television right now," he said. From billboards and bus advertisements, he was aware of the existence of a series named *Interstellar Boys*, but he wasn't familiar enough with it to recognize the cast members.

"She's the hot little blonde thing. Come on. You've seen her," Toby said.

"The girl in the bumblebee dress?"

Jamie giggled. "Bumblebee dress," she said. "For gosh sakes, Vish, that's a Frederic Lanchin. It's couture." Jamie's Texas roots sometimes came out in unguarded moments, and she pronounced it "couchure."

"She's hot," Toby said.

"She is?" Vish spread a clean black cloth napkin on his tray and began arranging the tacos in what he hoped was an aesthetically pleasing display. "She seemed so young." He pictured the girl teetering on the railing, her round face and downy-chick hairstyle and baby-doll voice. The idea of her as an object of anyone's fierce passion seemed absurd, like lusting after a stuffed animal.

"Eighteen in six weeks, man. Six weeks. Can't wait."

"For what? So you can drool over her?" Jamie opened the oven door a crack, peeked in on whatever was still in there, closed it. "Kinda seems like you're doing plenty of that already, sugar."

"So I can drool after her legally. Without feeling creepy about it." Toby shrugged. "Biological imperative, babe."

Vish wasn't sure what that meant, and he wasn't sure the sentiment bore careful parsing, either. Freshly-loaded tray in hand, he glanced through the archway into the dining room. The pretty man was in his line of sight, deep in conversation with Maryanne and her husband. "Hey, do either of you know that guy talking to the hosts?"

Jamie glanced over and shrugged. "No idea. Why?"

"Not sure. He looks familiar, sort of. Like he's someone I'm supposed to know."

"He's foxy," Jamie said. She nudged her elbow into his ribs and winked. "Are you interested?"

"That's not why I was asking."

"No offense meant. Just checking. You keep to yourself so much it's hard to know where your interests lie."

Toby squinted at the man. "I think he's just some guy," he said at last.

That seemed to be the final word on the matter, so Vish headed out into the party once more.

CHAPTER TWO

THE PARTY DEFLATED shortly thereafter. Guests seeped out and slipped off into the night; the noise level ebbed. It was still before midnight when Jamie, Toby and Vish began loading foil-wrapped trays of leftovers into the stubby white company van.

The night air was a relief after the stuffy kitchen. Vish could smell hot grease and smoke clinging to his hair and clothes. The back of the van reeked of chorizo and corn oil.

Toby scrambled into the passenger seat. That meant Vish would be nestled in back with the leftovers. His stomach lurched.

"You won't need me to unload, will you?" he asked. "I'm opening the shop in the morning. Would you mind if I just took off from here?"

Jamie looked at him, confused. "You mean walk?"

"Just down the hill. I can catch a bus when I hit Hollywood."

"It's fine with me, but it's an awful long way to the beach. Let me drop you off at the shop. That'll get you a whole lot closer to your place."

"No, I'm fine. I could use some air," Vish said. "Is there anything I should know for tomorrow?"

Jamie thought for a moment. "Should be pretty straightforward. Someone's coming in for a tasting in the morning, but I left everything marked in the fridge. That's about it." She paused. "Are you absolutely sure I can't give you a ride? It's late. It might be dangerous."

"I'm sure. Exercise will do me some good." Jamie was right. It was a long way to Venice Beach, and the buses at night were infrequent and erratic, but the urge for solitude trumped that right now. "I'll see you on Monday, okay?"

"Sure thing, sugar. Thanks for all your help tonight." Jamie looked concerned, but not like she was going to push the issue. With a wave, she climbed up into the front seat.

Jamie and Toby drove off down the canyon road. Vish followed on foot. No sidewalk, so he kept to the gravel shoulder. The road was narrow and twisty and dark, the only illumination provided by the glow of the city below. A moonless night, the sky inky and impenetrable.

All was quiet. Rare to find this kind of tranquil darkness in the middle of Los Angeles. The air smelled good, like eucalyptus and lemon verbena and damp earth. Early September, and the air was crisp, but not chilly.

He heard a rustle in the shrubbery forming a loose barrier between the road and the steep slope of the canyon, a crunching of pebbles, a stirring of dead leaves. A coyote, maybe, one of the many that roamed the hills in packs, sometimes wandering into town and dragging off the occasional family pet. They avoided humans, Vish had heard, but all the same, he quickened his pace a little.

He was crossing beside a parked car, something sleek and sumptuous, when he heard a voice: "Hey."

He turned. Leaning against the hood, arms folded across his chest, was the pretty man. Vish could barely see him in the darkness. "You didn't park on the hill?" the man asked.

"Hey. No, I'm catching the bus," Vish said. He paused. "Car trouble?"

The man shrugged. "Can't get it to start."

"What's wrong with it?" Vish asked. Not that he'd have any idea how to fix it, but it seemed only polite to ask.

Another shrug. "Not sure. I'm not really a car person, you know? Never had the interest." He straightened up, popped the hood. Gestured for Vish to look closer. "At a guess, though, I'd say this might be the problem."

A chaos of smashed parts. It looked like someone had wielded a sledgehammer and bashed everything, all that finely-tuned German engineering, into crushed bits. "Wow," Vish said. He looked at the man. "Who did that?"

"Don't know." He smiled. Very white teeth, shining in the darkness. His incisors were too long, giving him the impression of fangs. "I probably deserved it, though."

He said it in such a matter-of-fact way that Vish wasn't sure he was joking. There was something frightening about this level of destruction, that someone had directed so much rage and fury toward him in this specific manner. Cars were an extension of everyone's personalities here in Los Angeles. In the eyes of many, Vish's lack of his own car marked him as somehow incomplete, less than a wholly functioning human being. The attack on the car was an attack on the man.

Vish glanced around. The rustling in the bushes, the dark night, the empty road… "Do you want me to call you a cab?"

"A friend's picking me up. Thanks, though." The man looked thoughtful, but not worried.

All of a sudden, Vish felt... not scared, exactly, but something in that area. The man seemed defenseless, waiting by himself beside his ruined car with an unidentified enemy somewhere out there. He hesitated, then made the offer. "I could wait with you."

The man looked at him, his expression blank, and for a moment Vish thought he'd said something to offend him. Then he nodded. "Sure. If you wouldn't mind. Thanks. I was getting bored." He slammed down the hood and boosted himself up onto it. "Grab a seat."

Vish hesitated. "I don't want to destroy any fingerprints."

"Doesn't matter. Destroy away. I'm not going to report this."

Vish sat on the hood next to him. The car looked clean—shiny and freshly waxed, in fact—and if the man could trust his expensive suit to it, Vish didn't need to fret too much about getting his cheap work slacks dirty. "You really don't know who did this?"

"I can think of a few possibilities. A lot of people don't like me."

"I don't know who you are," Vish said. "It seems like I should, but I don't."

"No reason you should. Our social circles probably haven't overlapped much." The man extended a hand. "I'm Sparky."

"Vish." They shook.

"Fish?" Sparky asked. "Like... fish?" He made a little swimming motion with his hand.

"Vish. With a 'v'."

"Short for?" Sparky's expression was sharp, like it mattered.

"Viswanathan."

Sparky smiled. "I was hoping for Vicious. Or maybe Vishnu," he said. "Viswanathan? Isn't that a last name?"

"It's my mother's maiden name. Actually, it's my middle name, but I don't like my given name."

"Which is?"

"Michael."

Sparky stared at him as if he was trying to decide if Vish was making fun of him. It was an expression Vish saw a lot. Then he shook his head.

"So it's been established you're not an actor. Proceeding on the assumption you're not a career caterer, either, I'm guessing you're the other one." Off Vish's confused look, he elaborated: "Writer."

"Ah. Yes. I am. Trying to be one, at least."

"Screenplays?"

"Yes. I've just started, though. I'm not sure I have the hang of it yet."

"How long have you been in L.A.?" Sparky asked.

"A year, almost. I moved out from New York. I was a contributing editor at an online literary magazine, but it folded last year."

"So you moved out here. To write screenplays."

Was there a note of scorn in his tone, or was Vish overly sensitive on the issue? "Yeah, pretty much. You're in the entertainment industry?"

"Here? Who isn't?" Sparky smiled. "I'm on the management end of things. Nothing terribly glamorous." He propped his elbows against the windshield of the car and leaned back, staring up at the moonless sky. "You have any scripts you're shopping around?"

Idle curiosity, or genuine interest? "Nothing I'm happy with. Mostly I'm trying to get my book published."

A quick glance over at him. "Agent?"

Vish paused. "Ah… not right now. I had one in New York, but it didn't work out."

"Tell me about your book," Sparky said. "Pitch it to me. Really sell me on it."

Crud. Vish hated this kind of thing. Talking about himself made him self-conscious enough. Talking himself up, trying to make himself sound exciting and compelling and dynamic, made his soul wither and die. He took a deep breath and tried to arrange his thoughts.

"It's fiction, though it's sort of loosely based on my mother's life. She passed away last year." Sparky made some faint sympathetic noise at this, but said nothing. Vish continued. "She grew up in India and came to the United States and became a cardiologist. My book begins right after she started her internship at a hospital in Detroit."

He warmed to his narrative, gaining confidence, adding more and more details. Sparky's expression showed reassuring interest; he nodded in the right spots, silently encouraging Vish to go on.

When Vish finished, there was an odd moment of silence. Sparky smiled at him. "Sounds awful," he said.

His tone was so polite and cheery that for a moment Vish thought he had misheard. Before he could say anything, Sparky continued. "I mean, it's probably good. Well-written, at least. You seem smart, and you have a good grasp of the basic components of a story, and I have no doubt you can string words together in a pleasing manner. But seriously, it sounds like something I'd need to be paid to read."

225

He didn't need to sound so chipper about it. Vish swallowed once. "Okay. Thank you," he said.

Sparky gave him a sidelong look. "That's not much of a defense," he said.

"If it's not your kind of book, it's not your kind of book. There's no sense in me arguing the point."

"You're doing this all wrong, you know." Another smile. "This is the part where you tell me why this *should* be my kind of book. Turn on the charm. Sell yourself. Flirt with me, if applicable. Because if you're at all perceptive, and I think you probably are, you've picked up on clues that I might be someone important."

"I've made a note of that, yes."

"So…?"

"So I'm not comfortable promoting myself, that's all."

"You're in the wrong industry, then," Sparky said. "Nothing ventured, nothing gained, right?"

"I've ventured. Believe me, I've ventured. And I've never gained, have never even come close to gaining. Nothing's ever come of anything I've tried, and I've always ended up feeling cheap and ridiculous for the effort." It came out a bit sharper than he'd intended. Hard to tell in the darkness, but he thought Sparky looked surprised.

"So what's the plan then, Vish?" A note of something new in Sparky's voice, something slinky and coy slithering in beneath the sardonic bonhomie. "Keep serving shitty food to the beautiful people at parties until a handsome stranger offers you fame and fortune on a silver tray?"

Ah. Sparky was playing with him. Sparky might also be kind of an asshole. He was bored and killing time, and he had nothing to give him. Vish almost smiled, suddenly more at ease. Assholes

226

he could handle. "I suppose, if you're offering," he said. "Want to be my fairy godfather, Sparky?"

Another flash of those overlong incisors. Sparky was prettier when he didn't smile. "So you can flirt. I'd wondered." He sat upright. "Send me your book. I'll go through it, and we'll see what can be done."

"You already said you won't like it," Vish said. It came out a little bitchy.

"Doesn't matter. I don't have to like it. We'll do what we need to find a market for it." Sparky fished around in his wallet and produced a business card. He handed it to Vish. "That's my office. I'll be in on Monday."

Vish glanced at the card. Sparky Mother, it read, with a telephone number. No title, no company name. It also had a little line drawing on it, a fuzzy blue cartoon tiger holding a sparkler.

It was far and away the dumbest business card Vish had ever seen.

"Okay. Thanks," he said. He stuffed the card in his pants pocket. This was confusing. Was Sparky agreeing to take on his book, despite his clear antipathy toward it? What did he do, exactly? He'd said he was a manager... no, he'd said he was on the management side, which wasn't quite the same thing.

Sparky grinned. "You're not going to call me, are you?"

"I don't know," Vish said. "Maybe, maybe not. I don't know anything about you."

"So Google me. That's a good place to start. See what you think after that." Sparky shrugged. "I can do amazing things with you, if you've got the balls to let me."

Bit of a taunt there. Unmistakable. "We'll see."

"We surely will." Sparky nodded toward the curved road, where an approaching pair of headlights sliced through the darkness. "That's my ride."

A black sports car pulled onto the shoulder just ahead of them. Sparky slid off the hood of his own car and ambled over to the driver's side.

A tinted window rolled down. An Asian woman, Korean maybe, with bobbed copper hair and huge gold hoop earrings looked up at Sparky from underneath a thick sheaf of glossy bangs. "Hey, you," she said. "Hop in. They'll tow you in the morning."

"Thanks, Poppy. Poppy, this is Vish." Sparky beckoned him over. "He was nice enough to keep me company, I figure the least we can do is give him a ride home." He turned to Vish. "Where do you live?"

Poppy glanced at Vish. She was extremely pretty and extremely made-up. Eyes lined in a thick layer of smudgy black, lashes long and spiky. She wore a gold tank dress covered in large sequins that glittered when she moved.

While Sparky's attention was on Vish, she caught his eye and shook her head, just a fraction of an inch, once.

Ah. "Don't worry about it," Vish said. "The bus is fine. Thanks anyway."

Sparky frowned. "You sure?" he asked. "We can at least run you down the hill to your bus stop."

"I need the walk," Vish said. He'd grown a little cold sitting in the night air with Sparky, and his white button-down shirt and the dumb red polyester vest Jamie made all her employees wear so they'd look like a cohesive team weren't providing much warmth. A ride would be nice, actually, but Poppy had sent him a very clear signal he shouldn't take Sparky up on his offer. "Hollywood isn't far from here."

"Suit yourself," Sparky said. He stuck out his hand. "Good meeting you, Vish. And thanks."

"Sure." They shook. Sparky's nails were manicured; the white cuff that stuck out from beneath his suit coat was crisp and immaculate. Diamond cufflinks glittered.

"Call me Monday, right? We'll talk," Sparky said. He sauntered around the front of the car and slid into the passenger seat.

With a quick nod at Vish, Poppy pulled forward, flipped a u-turn in the middle of the road, and headed down the hill.

Vish followed at a slow walk. As soon as Poppy's car rounded the first turn, the lights from the taillights vanished, leaving him alone in the dark.

ACKNOWLEDGMENTS

I owe a huge debt of gratitude to my crackerjack proofreading team of Sammy Woogerd, Jennifer DeBord, and Jenny Elliott, each of whom spotted errors that would've otherwise slipped right past me. Big thanks are also due to Elsbeth Monnett for painting that gorgeous cover image and to my longtime graphic design guru Morgan Dodge for holding my hand through the whole gnarly ordeal of putting the cover together. Thanks also go to my sister Ingrid for the moral support, to Joe Richter for saying such nice things about *Wrong City*, and to R. Diskin Black for buying all the margaritas.

ABOUT THE AUTHOR

A graduate of the screenwriting program at USC's film school, Morgan Richter has worked in production on several TV shows, including *Talk Soup* and *America's Funniest Home Videos*, and has contributed pop culture reviews and essays to websites such as TVgasm and Forces of Geek, as well as to her own site, Preppies of the Apocalypse. She is the author of *Bias Cut*, *Lonely Satellite*, *Charlotte Dent*, and *Wrong City*. *Bias Cut* won a silver medal in the Mystery category at the 2013 Independent Publisher Book Awards and was a 2012 semi-finalist for the Amazon Breakthrough Novel Award (ABNA). *Charlotte Dent* was a 2008 ABNA semi-finalist; *Lonely Satellite* was a 2014 ABNA quarter-finalist. Born and raised in Spokane, Washington, she currently lives in New York City.